A CLASSIC CHRISTMAS TREASURY

ROCK
POINT

First published in 2023 by Rock Point, an imprint of The Quarto Group,
142 West 36th Street, 4th Floor, New York, NY 10018, USA
T (212) 779-4972 F (212) 779-6058 www.Quarto.com

Rock Point titles are also available at discount for retail, wholesale, promotional, and bulk purchase. For details, contact the Special Sales Manager by email at specialsales@quarto.com or by mail at The Quarto Group, Attn: Special Sales Manager, 100 Cummings Center Suite 265D, Beverly, MA 01915 USA.

10 9 8 7 6 5 4 3 2 1

ISBN: 978-1-63106-984-0

Library of Congress Control Number: 2023936520

Publisher: Rage Kindelsperger
Creative Director: Laura Drew
Managing Editor: Cara Donaldson
Editorial Assistant: Zoe Briscoe
Cover Design: Beth Middleworth

Printed in China

Contents

JOY TO THE WORLD
A Letter from the Editors

The wintry tales included in this curated holiday collection are absolute delights, ones we recommend best enjoyed with candy canes and cocoa. These eclectic stories come to us from around the world, but all share the gift of unforgettable lessons. From empathizing with those less fortunate to appreciating the complexities of other languages to remembering authors who have been historically excluded, these tales—some familiar and others new to discover—will linger in your mind as well as your heart for seasons to come.

Enjoy this beautiful collection of festive stories, and don't forget to share the wonderful wisdom and gifts of the holiday season with the people you love all days of the year.

THE TWELVE DAYS OF CHRISTMAS

Unison

English traditional
(G.H.)

A CHRISTMAS CAROL

By Charles Dickens

PREFACE

I have endeavoured in this Ghostly little book to raise the Ghost of an Idea which shall not put my readers out of humour with themselves, with each other, with the season, or with me. May it haunt their house pleasantly, and no one wish to lay it.

Their faithful Friend and Servant,

C. D.

December, 1843.

CHARACTERS

Bob Cratchit, clerk to Ebenezer Scrooge.

Peter Cratchit, a son of the preceding.

Tim Cratchit ("Tiny Tim"), a cripple, youngest son of Bob Cratchit.

Mr. Fezziwig, a kind-hearted, jovial old merchant.

Fred, Scrooge's nephew.

Ghost of Christmas Past, a phantom showing things past.

Ghost of Christmas Present, a spirit of a kind, generous, and hearty nature.

Ghost of Christmas Yet to Come, an apparition showing the shadows of things which yet may happen.

Ghost of Jacob Marley, a spectre of Scrooge's former partner in business.

Joe, a marine-store dealer and receiver of stolen goods.

Ebenezer Scrooge, a grasping, covetous old man, the surviving partner of the firm of Scrooge and Marley.

Mr. Topper, a bachelor.

Dick Wilkins, a fellow apprentice of Scrooge's.

Belle, a comely matron, an old sweetheart of Scrooge's.

Caroline, wife of one of Scrooge's debtors.

Mrs. Cratchit, wife of Bob Cratchit.

Belinda and Martha Cratchit, daughters of the preceding.

Mrs. Dilber, a laundress.

Fan, the sister of Scrooge.

Mrs. Fezziwig, the worthy partner of Mr. Fezziwig.

PART ONE

Marley's Ghost

Marley was dead, to begin with. There is no doubt whatever about that. The register of his burial was signed by the clergyman, the clerk, the undertaker, and the chief mourner. Scrooge signed it. And Scrooge's name was good upon 'Change for anything he chose to put his hand to. Old Marley was as dead as a door-nail.

Mind! I don't mean to say that I know of my own knowledge, what there is particularly dead about a door-nail. I might have been inclined, myself, to regard a coffin-nail as the deadest piece of ironmongery in the trade. But the wisdom of our ancestors is in the simile; and my unhallowed hands shall not disturb it, or the country's done for. You will, therefore, permit me to repeat, emphatically, that Marley was as dead as a door-nail.

Scrooge knew he was dead? Of course he did. How could it be otherwise? Scrooge and he were partners for I don't know how many years. Scrooge was his sole executor, his sole administrator, his sole assign, his sole residuary legatee, his sole friend, and sole mourner. And even Scrooge was not so dreadfully cut up by the sad event but that he was an excellent man of business on the very day of the funeral, and solemnised it with an undoubted bargain.

The mention of Marley's funeral brings me back to the point I started from. There is no doubt that Marley was dead. This must be distinctly understood, or nothing wonderful can come of the story I am going to relate. If we were not perfectly convinced that Hamlet's father died before the play began, there would be nothing more remarkable in his taking a stroll at night, in an easterly wind, upon his own ramparts, than there would be in any other middle-aged gentleman rashly turning out after dark in a breezy spot—say St. Paul's Churchyard, for instance—literally to astonish his son's weak mind.

Scrooge never painted out Old Marley's name. There it stood, years afterwards, above the warehouse door: Scrooge and Marley. The firm was known as Scrooge and Marley. Sometimes people new to the business called Scrooge Scrooge, and sometimes Marley, but he answered to both names. It was all the same to him.

Oh! but he was a tight-fisted hand at the grindstone, Scrooge! a squeezing, wrenching, grasping, scraping, clutching, covetous old sinner! Hard and sharp as flint, from which no steel had ever struck out generous fire; secret, and self-contained, and solitary as an oyster. The cold within him froze his old features, nipped his pointed nose, shrivelled his cheek, stiffened his gait; made his eyes red, his thin lips blue; and spoke out shrewdly in his grating voice. A frosty rime was on his head, and on his eyebrows, and his wiry chin. He carried his own low temperature always about with him; he iced his office in the dog-days, and didn't thaw it one degree at Christmas.

External heat and cold had little influence on Scrooge. No warmth could warm, no wintry weather chill him. No wind that blew was bitterer than he, no falling snow was more intent upon its purpose, no pelting rain less open to entreaty. Foul weather didn't know where to have him. The heaviest rain, and snow, and hail, and sleet could boast of the advantage over him in only one respect. They often 'came down' handsomely, and Scrooge never did.

Nobody ever stopped him in the street to say, with gladsome looks, 'My dear Scrooge, how are you? When will you come to see me?' No beggars implored him to bestow a trifle, no children asked him what it was o'clock, no man or woman ever once in all his life inquired the way to such and such a place, of Scrooge. Even the blind men's dogs appeared to know him; and, when they saw him coming on, would tug their owners into doorways and up courts; and then would wag their tails as though they said, 'No eye at all is better than an evil eye, dark master!'

But what did Scrooge care? It was the very thing he liked. To edge his way along the crowded paths of life, warning all human sympathy to keep its distance, was what the knowing ones call 'nuts' to Scrooge.

Once upon a time—of all the good days in the year, on Christmas Eve—old Scrooge sat busy in his counting-house. It was cold, bleak, biting weather; foggy withal; and he could hear the people in the court outside go wheezing up and down, beating their hands upon their breasts, and stamping their feet upon the pavement stones to warm them. The City clocks had only just gone three, but it was quite dark already—it had not been light all day—and candles were flaring in the windows of the neighbouring offices, like ruddy smears upon the palpable brown air. The fog came pouring in at every chink and keyhole, and was so dense without, that, although the court was of the narrowest, the houses opposite were mere phantoms. To see the dingy cloud come drooping down, obscuring everything, one might have thought that nature lived hard by, and was brewing on a large scale.

The door of Scrooge's counting-house was open, that he might keep his eye upon his clerk, who in a dismal little cell beyond, a sort of tank, was copying letters. Scrooge had a very small fire, but the clerk's fire was so very much smaller that it looked like one coal. But he couldn't replenish it, for Scrooge kept the coal-box in his own room; and so surely as the clerk came in with the shovel, the master predicted that it would be necessary for them to part. Wherefore the clerk put on his white comforter, and tried to warm himself at the candle; in which effort, not being a man of strong imagination, he failed.

'A merry Christmas, uncle! God save you!' cried a cheerful voice. It was the voice of Scrooge's nephew, who came upon him so quickly that this was the first intimation he had of his approach.

'Bah!' said Scrooge. 'Humbug!'

He had so heated himself with rapid walking in the fog and frost, this nephew of Scrooge's, that he was all in a glow; his face was ruddy and handsome; his eyes sparkled, and his breath smoked again.

'Christmas a humbug, uncle!' said Scrooge's nephew. 'You don't mean that, I am sure?'

'I do,' said Scrooge. 'Merry Christmas! What right have you to be merry? What reason have you to be merry? You're poor enough.'

'Come, then,' returned the nephew gaily. 'What right have you to be dismal? What reason have you to be morose? You're rich enough.'

Scrooge, having no better answer ready on the spur of the moment, said, 'Bah!' again; and followed it up with 'Humbug!'

'Don't be cross, uncle!' said the nephew.

'What else can I be,' returned the uncle, 'when I live in such a world of fools as this? Merry Christmas! Out upon merry Christmas! What's Christmas-time to you but a time for paying bills without money; a time for finding yourself a year older, and not an hour richer; a time for balancing your books, and having every item in 'em through a round dozen of months presented dead against you? If I could work my will,' said Scrooge indignantly, 'every idiot who goes about with, "Merry Christmas" on his lips should be boiled with his own pudding, and buried with a stake of holly through his heart. He should!'

'Uncle!' pleaded the nephew.

'Nephew!' returned the uncle sternly, 'keep Christmas in your own way, and let me keep it in mine.'

'Keep it!' repeated Scrooge's nephew. 'But you don't keep it.'

'Let me leave it alone, then,' said Scrooge. 'Much good may it do you! Much good it has ever done you!'

'There are many things from which I might have derived good, by which I have not profited, I dare say,' returned the nephew; 'Christmas among the rest. But I am sure I have always thought of Christmas-time, when it has come round—apart from the veneration due to its sacred name and origin, if anything belonging to it can be apart from that—as a good time; a kind, forgiving, charitable, pleasant time; the only time I know of, in the long calendar of the year, when men and women seem by one consent to open their shut-up hearts freely, and to think of people below them as if they really were fellow-passengers to the grave, and not another race of creatures bound on other journeys. And therefore, uncle, though it has never put a scrap of gold or silver in my pocket, I believe that it *has* done me good and *will* do me good; and I say, God bless it!'

The clerk in the tank involuntarily applauded. Becoming immediately sensible of the impropriety, he poked the fire, and extinguished the last frail spark for ever.

'Let me hear another sound from *you*,' said Scrooge, 'and you'll keep your Christmas by losing your situation! You're quite a powerful speaker, sir,' he added, turning to his nephew. 'I wonder you don't go into Parliament.'

'Don't be angry, uncle. Come! Dine with us tomorrow.'

Scrooge said that he would see him——Yes, indeed he did. He went the whole length of the expression, and said that he would see him in that extremity first.

'But why?' cried Scrooge's nephew. 'Why?'

'Why did you get married?' said Scrooge.

'Because I fell in love.'

'Because you fell in love!' growled Scrooge, as if that were the only one thing in the world more ridiculous than a merry Christmas. 'Good afternoon!'

'Nay, uncle, but you never came to see me before that happened. Why give it as a reason for not coming now?'

'Good afternoon,' said Scrooge.

'I want nothing from you; I ask nothing of you; why cannot we be friends?'

'Good afternoon!' said Scrooge.

'I am sorry, with all my heart, to find you so resolute. We have never had any quarrel to which I have been a party. But I have made the trial in homage to Christmas, and I'll keep my Christmas humour to the last. So A Merry Christmas, uncle!'

'Good afternoon,' said Scrooge.

'And A Happy New Year!'

'Good afternoon!' said Scrooge.

His nephew left the room without an angry word, notwithstanding. He stopped at the outer door to bestow the greetings of the season on the clerk, who, cold as he was, was warmer than Scrooge; for he returned them cordially.

'There's another fellow,' muttered Scrooge, who overheard him: 'my clerk, with fifteen shillings a week, and a wife and family, talking about a merry Christmas. I'll retire to Bedlam.'

This lunatic, in letting Scrooge's nephew out, had let two other people in. They were portly gentlemen, pleasant to behold, and now stood, with their hats off, in Scrooge's office. They had books and papers in their hands, and bowed to him.

'Scrooge and Marley's, I believe,' said one of the gentlemen, referring to his list. 'Have I the pleasure of addressing Mr. Scrooge, or Mr. Marley?'

'Mr. Marley has been dead these seven years,' Scrooge replied. 'He died seven years ago, this very night.'

'We have no doubt his liberality is well represented by his surviving partner,' said the gentleman, presenting his credentials.

It certainly was; for they had been two kindred spirits. At the ominous word 'liberality' Scrooge frowned, and shook his head, and handed the credentials back.

'At this festive season of the year, Mr. Scrooge,' said the gentleman, taking up a pen, 'it is more than usually desirable that we should make some slight provision for the poor and destitute, who suffer greatly at the present time. Many thousands are in want of common necessaries; hundreds of thousands are in want of common comforts, sir.'

'Are there no prisons?' asked Scrooge.

'Plenty of prisons,' said the gentleman, laying down the pen again.

'And the Union workhouses?' demanded Scrooge. 'Are they still in operation?'

'They are. Still,' returned the gentleman, 'I wish I could say they were not.'

'The Treadmill and the Poor Law are in full vigour, then?' said Scrooge.

'Both very busy, sir.'

'Oh! I was afraid, from what you said at first, that something had occurred to stop them in their useful course,' said Scrooge. 'I am very glad to hear it.'

'Under the impression that they scarcely furnish Christian cheer of mind or body to the multitude,' returned the gentleman, 'a few of us are endeavouring to raise a fund to buy the Poor some meat and drink, and means of warmth. We choose this time, because it is a time, of all others, when Want is keenly felt, and Abundance rejoices. What shall I put you down for?'

'Nothing!' Scrooge replied.

'You wish to be anonymous?'

'I wish to be left alone,' said Scrooge. 'Since you ask me what I wish, gentlemen, that is my answer. I don't make merry myself at Christmas, and I can't afford to make idle people merry. I help to support the establishments I have mentioned—they cost enough: and those who are badly off must go there.'

'Many can't go there; and many would rather die.'

'If they would rather die,' said Scrooge, 'they had better do it, and decrease the surplus population. Besides—excuse me—I don't know that.'

'But you might know it,' observed the gentleman.

'It's not my business,' Scrooge returned. 'It's enough for a man to understand his own business, and not to interfere with other people's. Mine occupies me constantly. Good afternoon, gentlemen!'

Seeing clearly that it would be useless to pursue their point, the gentlemen withdrew. Scrooge resumed his labours with an improved opinion of himself, and in a more facetious temper than was usual with him.

Meanwhile the fog and darkness thickened so, that people ran about with flaring links, proffering their services to go before horses in carriages, and conduct them on their way. The ancient tower of a church, whose gruff old bell was always peeping slily down at Scrooge out of a Gothic window in the wall, became invisible, and struck the hours and quarters in the clouds, with tremulous vibrations afterwards, as if its teeth were chattering in its frozen head up there. The cold became intense. In the main street, at the corner of the court, some labourers were repairing the gas-pipes, and had lighted a great fire in a brazier, round which a party of ragged men and boys were gathered: warming their hands and winking their eyes before the blaze in rapture. The water-plug being left in solitude, its overflowings suddenly congealed, and turned to misanthropic ice. The brightness of the shops, where holly sprigs and berries crackled in the lamp heat of the windows, made pale faces ruddy as they passed. Poulterers' and grocers' trades became a splendid joke: a glorious pageant, with which it was next to impossible to believe that such dull principles as bargain and sale had anything to do. The Lord Mayor, in the stronghold of the mighty Mansion House, gave orders to his fifty cooks and butlers to keep Christmas as a Lord Mayor's household should; and even the little tailor, whom he had fined five shillings on the previous Monday for being drunk and bloodthirsty in the streets, stirred up tomorrow's pudding in his garret, while his lean wife and the baby sallied out to buy the beef.

Foggier yet, and colder! Piercing, searching, biting cold. If the good St. Dunstan had but nipped the Evil Spirit's nose with a touch of such weather as that, instead of using his familiar weapons, then indeed he would have roared to lusty purpose. The owner of one scant young nose, gnawed and mumbled by the hungry cold as bones are gnawed by dogs, stooped down at Scrooge's keyhole to regale him with a Christmas carol; but, at the first sound of

'God bless you, merry gentleman,

May nothing you dismay!'

Scrooge seized the ruler with such energy of action that the singer fled in terror, leaving the keyhole to the fog, and even more congenial frost.

At length the hour of shutting up the counting-house arrived. With an ill-will Scrooge dismounted from his stool, and tacitly admitted the fact to the expectant clerk in the tank, who instantly snuffed his candle out, and put on his hat.

'You'll want all day tomorrow, I suppose?' said Scrooge.

'If quite convenient, sir.'

'It's not convenient,' said Scrooge, 'and it's not fair. If I was to stop half-a-crown for it, you'd think yourself ill used, I'll be bound?'

The clerk smiled faintly.

'And yet,' said Scrooge, 'you don't think me ill used when I pay a day's wages for no work.'

The clerk observed that it was only once a year.

'A poor excuse for picking a man's pocket every twenty-fifth of December!' said Scrooge, buttoning his greatcoat to the chin. 'But I suppose you must have the whole day. Be here all the earlier next morning.'

The clerk promised that he would; and Scrooge walked out with a growl. The office was closed in a twinkling, and the clerk, with the long ends of his white comforter dangling below his waist (for he boasted no greatcoat), went down a slide on Cornhill, at the end of a lane of boys, twenty times, in honour of its being Christmas Eve, and then ran home to Camden Town as hard as he could pelt, to play at blindman's-buff.

Scrooge took his melancholy dinner in his usual melancholy tavern; and having read all the newspapers, and beguiled the rest of the evening with his banker's book, went home to bed. He lived in chambers which had once belonged to his deceased partner. They were a gloomy suite of rooms, in a lowering pile of building up a yard, where it had so little business to be, that one could scarcely help fancying it must have run there when it was a young house, playing at hide-and-seek with other houses, and have forgotten the way out again. It was old enough now, and dreary enough; for nobody lived in it but Scrooge, the other rooms being all let out as offices. The yard was so dark that even Scrooge, who knew its every stone, was fain to grope with his hands. The fog and frost so hung about the black old gateway of the house, that it seemed as if the Genius of the Weather sat in mournful meditation on the threshold.

Now, it is a fact that there was nothing at all particular about the knocker on the door, except that it was very large. It is also a fact that Scrooge had seen it, night and morning, during his whole residence in that place; also that Scrooge had as little of what is called fancy about him as any man in the City of London, even including—which is a bold word—the corporation, aldermen, and livery. Let it also be borne in mind that Scrooge had not bestowed one thought on Marley since his last mention of his seven-years'-dead partner that afternoon. And then let any man explain to me, if he can, how it happened that Scrooge, having his key in the lock of the door, saw in the knocker, without its undergoing any intermediate process of change—not a knocker, but Marley's face.

Marley's face. It was not in impenetrable shadow, as the other objects in the yard were, but had a dismal light about it, like a bad lobster in a dark cellar. It was not angry or ferocious, but looked at Scrooge as Marley used to look; with ghostly spectacles turned up on its ghostly forehead. The hair was curiously stirred, as if by breath or hot air; and, though the eyes were wide open, they were perfectly motionless. That, and its livid colour, made it horrible; but its horror seemed to be in spite of the face, and beyond its controul, rather than a part of its own expression.

As Scrooge looked fixedly at this phenomenon, it was a knocker again.

To say that he was not startled, or that his blood was not conscious of a terrible sensation to which it had been a stranger from infancy, would be untrue. But he put his hand upon the key he had relinquished, turned it sturdily, walked in, and lighted his candle.

He *did* pause, with a moment's irresolution, before he shut the door; and he *did* look cautiously behind it first, as if he half expected to be terrified with the sight of Marley's pigtail sticking out into the hall. But there was nothing on the back of the door, except the screws and nuts that held the knocker on, so he said, 'Pooh, pooh!' and closed it with a bang.

The sound resounded through the house like thunder. Every room above, and every cask in the wine-merchant's cellars below, appeared to have a separate peal of echoes of its own. Scrooge was not a man to be frightened by echoes. He fastened the door, and walked across the hall, and up the stairs: slowly, too: trimming his candle as he went.

You may talk vaguely about driving a coach and six up a good old flight of stairs, or through a bad young Act of Parliament; but I mean to say you might have got a hearse up that staircase, and taken it broadwise, with the splinter-bar towards the wall, and the door towards the balustrades: and done it easy. There was plenty of width for that, and room to spare; which is perhaps the reason why Scrooge thought he saw a locomotive hearse going on before him in the gloom. Half-a-dozen gas-lamps out of the street wouldn't have lighted the entry too well, so you may suppose that it was pretty dark with Scrooge's dip.

Up Scrooge went, not caring a button for that. Darkness is cheap, and Scrooge liked it. But, before he shut his heavy door, he walked through his rooms to see that all was right. He had just enough recollection of the face to desire to do that.

Sitting-room, bedroom, lumber-room. All as they should be. Nobody under the table, nobody under the sofa; a small fire in the grate; spoon and basin ready; and the little saucepan of gruel (Scrooge had a cold in his head) upon the hob. Nobody under the bed; nobody in the closet; nobody in his dressing-gown, which was hanging up in a suspicious attitude against the wall. Lumber-room as usual. Old fire-guard, old shoes, two fish baskets, washing-stand on three legs, and a poker.

Quite satisfied, he closed his door, and locked himself in; double locked himself in, which was not his custom. Thus secured against surprise, he took off his cravat; put on his dressing-gown and slippers, and his nightcap; and sat down before the fire to take his gruel.

It was a very low fire indeed; nothing on such a bitter night. He was obliged to sit close to it, and brood over it, before he could extract the least sensation of warmth from such a handful of fuel. The fireplace was an old one, built by some Dutch merchant long ago, and paved all round with quaint Dutch tiles, designed to illustrate the Scriptures. There were Cains and Abels, Pharaoh's daughters, Queens of Sheba, Angelic messengers descending through the air on clouds like feather-beds, Abrahams, Belshazzars, Apostles putting off to sea in butter-boats, hundreds of figures to attract his thoughts; and yet that face of Marley, seven years dead, came like the ancient Prophet's rod, and swallowed up the whole. If each smooth tile had been a blank at first, with power to shape some picture on its surface from the disjointed fragments of his thoughts, there would have been a copy of old Marley's head on every one.

'Humbug!' said Scrooge; and walked across the room.

After several turns he sat down again. As he threw his head back in the chair, his glance happened to rest upon a bell, a disused bell, that hung in the room, and communicated, for some purpose now forgotten, with a chamber in the highest storey of the building. It was with great astonishment, and with a strange, inexplicable dread, that, as he looked, he saw this bell begin to swing. It swung so softly in the outset that it scarcely made a sound; but soon it rang out loudly, and so did every bell in the house.

This might have lasted half a minute, or a minute, but it seemed an hour. The bells ceased, as they had begun, together. They were succeeded by a clanking noise deep down below as if some person were dragging a heavy chain over the casks in the wine-merchant's cellar. Scrooge then remembered to have heard that ghosts in haunted houses were described as dragging chains.

The cellar door flew open with a booming sound, and then he heard the noise much louder on the floors below; then coming up the stairs; then coming straight towards his door.

'It's humbug still!' said Scrooge. 'I won't believe it.'

His colour changed, though, when, without a pause, it came on through the heavy door and passed into the room before his eyes. Upon its coming in, the dying flame leaped up, as though it cried, 'I know him! Marley's Ghost!' and fell again.

The same face: the very same. Marley in his pigtail, usual waistcoat, tights, and boots; the tassels on the latter bristling, like his pigtail, and his coat-skirts, and the hair upon his head. The chain he drew was clasped about his middle. It was long, and wound about him like a tail; and it was made (for Scrooge observed it closely) of cash-boxes, keys, padlocks, ledgers, deeds, and heavy purses wrought in steel. His body was transparent: so that Scrooge, observing him, and looking through his waistcoat, could see the two buttons on his coat behind.

Scrooge had often heard it said that Marley had no bowels, but he had never believed it until now.

No, nor did he believe it even now. Though he looked the phantom through and through, and saw it standing before him; though he felt the chilling influence of its death-cold eyes, and marked the very texture of the folded kerchief bound about its head and chin, which wrapper he had not observed before, he was still incredulous, and fought against his senses.

'How now!' said Scrooge, caustic and cold as ever. 'What do you want with me?'

'Much!'—Marley's voice; no doubt about it.

'Who are you?'

'Ask me who I *was*.'

'Who *were* you, then?' said Scrooge, raising his voice. 'You're particular, for a shade.' He was going to say '*to* a shade,' but substituted this, as more appropriate.

'In life I was your partner, Jacob Marley.'

'Can you—can you sit down?' asked Scrooge, looking doubtfully at him.

'I can.'

'Do it, then.'

Scrooge asked the question, because he didn't know whether a ghost so transparent might find himself in a condition to take a chair; and felt that in the event of its being impossible, it might involve the necessity of an embarrassing explanation. But the Ghost sat down on the opposite side of the fireplace, as if he were quite used to it.

'You don't believe in me,' observed the Ghost.

'I don't,' said Scrooge.

'What evidence would you have of my reality beyond that of your own senses?'

'I don't know,' said Scrooge.

'Why do you doubt your senses?'

'Because,' said Scrooge, 'a little thing affects them. A slight disorder of the stomach makes them cheats. You may be an undigested bit of beef, a blot of mustard, a crumb of cheese, a fragment of an underdone potato. There's more of gravy than of grave about you, whatever you are!'

Scrooge was not much in the habit of cracking jokes, nor did he feel in his heart by any means waggish then. The truth is, that he tried to be smart, as a means of distracting his own attention, and keeping down his terror; for the spectre's voice disturbed the very marrow in his bones.

To sit staring at those fixed, glazed eyes in silence, for a moment, would play, Scrooge felt, the very deuce with him. There was something very awful, too, in the spectre's being provided with an infernal atmosphere of his own. Scrooge could not feel it himself, but this was clearly the case; for though the Ghost sat perfectly motionless, its hair, and skirts, and tassels were still agitated as by the hot vapour from an oven.

'You see this toothpick?' said Scrooge, returning quickly to the charge, for the reason just assigned; and wishing, though it were only for a second, to divert the vision's stony gaze from himself.

'I do,' replied the Ghost.

'You are not looking at it,' said Scrooge.

'But I see it,' said the Ghost, 'notwithstanding.'

'Well!' returned Scrooge, 'I have but to swallow this, and be for the rest of my days persecuted by a legion of goblins, all of my own creation. Humbug, I tell you: humbug!'

At this the spirit raised a frightful cry, and shook its chain with such a dismal and appalling noise, that Scrooge held on tight to his chair, to save himself from falling in a swoon. But how much greater was his horror when the phantom, taking off the bandage round his head, as if it were too warm to wear indoors, its lower jaw dropped down upon its breast!

Scrooge fell upon his knees, and clasped his hands before his face.

'Mercy!' he said. 'Dreadful apparition, why do you trouble me?'

'Man of the worldly mind!' replied the Ghost, 'do you believe in me or not?'

'I do,' said Scrooge; 'I must. But why do spirits walk the earth, and why do they come to me?'

'It is required of every man,' the Ghost returned, 'that the spirit within him should walk abroad among his fellow-men, and travel far and wide; and, if that spirit goes not forth in life, it is condemned to do so after death. It is doomed to wander through the world—oh, woe is me!—and witness what it cannot share, but might have shared on earth, and turned to happiness!'

Again the spectre raised a cry, and shook its chain and wrung its shadowy hands.

'You are fettered,' said Scrooge, trembling. 'Tell me why?'

'I wear the chain I forged in life,' replied the Ghost. 'I made it link by link, and yard by yard; I girded it on of my own free will, and of my own free will I wore it. Is its pattern strange to *you?*'

Scrooge trembled more and more.

'Or would you know,' pursued the Ghost, 'the weight and length of the strong coil you bear yourself? It was full as heavy and as long as this seven Christmas Eves ago. You have laboured on it since. It is a ponderous chain!'

Scrooge glanced about him on the floor, in the expectation of finding himself surrounded by some fifty or sixty fathoms of iron cable; but he could see nothing.

'Jacob!' he said imploringly. 'Old Jacob Marley, tell me more! Speak comfort to me, Jacob!'

'I have none to give,' the Ghost replied. 'It comes from other regions, Ebenezer Scrooge, and is conveyed by other ministers, to other kinds of men. Nor can I tell you what I would. A very little more is all permitted to me. I cannot rest, I cannot stay, I cannot linger anywhere. My spirit never walked beyond our counting-house—mark me;—in life my spirit never roved beyond the narrow limits of our money-changing hole; and weary journeys lie before me!'

It was a habit with Scrooge, whenever he became thoughtful, to put his hands in his breeches pockets. Pondering on what the Ghost had said, he did so now, but without lifting up his eyes, or getting off his knees.

'You must have been very slow about it, Jacob,' Scrooge observed in a business-like manner, though with humility and deference.

'Slow!' the Ghost repeated.

'Seven years dead,' mused Scrooge. 'And travelling all the time?'

'The whole time,' said the Ghost. 'No rest, no peace. Incessant torture of remorse.'

'You travel fast?' said Scrooge.

'On the wings of the wind,' replied the Ghost.

'You might have got over a great quantity of ground in seven years,' said Scrooge.

The Ghost, on hearing this, set up another cry, and clanked its chain so hideously in the dead silence of the night, that the Ward would have been justified in indicting it for a nuisance.

'Oh! captive, bound, and double-ironed,' cried the phantom, 'not to know that ages of incessant labour, by immortal creatures, for this earth must pass into eternity before the good of which it is susceptible is all developed! Not to know that any Christian spirit working kindly in its little sphere, whatever it may be, will find its mortal life too short for its vast means of usefulness! Not to know that no space of regret can make amends for one life's opportunities misused! Yet such was I! Oh, such was I!'

'But you were always a good man of business, Jacob,' faltered Scrooge, who now began to apply this to himself.

'Business!' cried the Ghost, wringing its hands again. 'Mankind was my business. The common welfare was my business; charity, mercy, forbearance, and benevolence were, all, my business. The dealings of my trade were but a drop of water in the comprehensive ocean of my business!'

It held up its chain at arm's-length, as if that were the cause of all its unavailing grief, and flung it heavily upon the ground again.

'At this time of the rolling year,' the spectre said, 'I suffer most. Why did I walk through crowds of fellow-beings with my eyes turned down, and never raise them to that blessed Star which led the Wise Men to a poor abode? Were there no poor homes to which its light would have conducted *me?*'

Scrooge was very much dismayed to hear the spectre going on at this rate, and began to quake exceedingly.

'Hear me!' cried the Ghost. 'My time is nearly gone.'

'I will,' said Scrooge. 'But don't be hard upon me! Don't be flowery, Jacob! Pray!'

'How it is that I appear before you in a shape that you can see, I may not tell. I have sat invisible beside you many and many a day.'

It was not an agreeable idea. Scrooge shivered, and wiped the perspiration from his brow.

'That is no light part of my penance,' pursued the Ghost. 'I am here tonight to warn you that you have yet a chance and hope of escaping my fate. A chance and hope of my procuring, Ebenezer.'

'You were always a good friend to me,' said Scrooge. 'Thankee!'

'You will be haunted,' resumed the Ghost, 'by Three Spirits.'

Scrooge's countenance fell almost as low as the Ghost's had done.

'Is that the chance and hope you mentioned, Jacob?' he demanded in a faltering voice.

'It is.'

'I—I think I'd rather not,' said Scrooge.

'Without their visits,' said the Ghost, 'you cannot hope to shun the path I tread. Expect the first tomorrow when the bell tolls One.'

'Couldn't I take 'em all at once, and have it over, Jacob?' hinted Scrooge.

'Expect the second on the next night at the same hour. The third, upon the next night when the last stroke of Twelve has ceased to vibrate. Look to see me no more; and look that, for your own sake, you remember what has passed between us!'

When it had said these words, the spectre took its wrapper from the table, and bound it round its head as before. Scrooge knew this by the smart sound its teeth made when the jaws were brought together by the bandage. He ventured to raise his eyes again, and found his supernatural visitor confronting him in an erect attitude, with its chain wound over and about its arm.

The apparition walked backward from him; and, at every step it took, the window raised itself a little, so that, when the spectre reached it, it was wide open. It beckoned Scrooge to approach, which he did. When they were within two paces of each other, Marley's Ghost held up its hand, warning him to come no nearer. Scrooge stopped.

Not so much in obedience as in surprise and fear; for, on the raising of the hand, he became sensible of confused noises in the air; incoherent sounds of lamentation and regret; wailings inexpressibly sorrowful and self-accusatory. The spectre, after listening for a moment, joined in the mournful dirge; and floated out upon the bleak, dark night.

Scrooge followed to the window: desperate in his curiosity. He looked out.

The air was filled with phantoms, wandering hither and thither in restless haste, and moaning as they went. Every one of them wore chains like Marley's Ghost; some few (they might be guilty governments) were linked together; none were free. Many had been personally known to Scrooge in their lives. He had been quite familiar with one old ghost in a white waistcoat, with a monstrous iron safe attached to its ankle, who cried piteously at being unable to assist a wretched woman with an infant, whom it saw below upon a doorstep. The misery with them all was clearly, that they sought to interfere, for good, in human matters, and had lost the power for ever.

Whether these creatures faded into mist, or mist enshrouded them, he could not tell. But they and their spirit voices faded together; and the night became as it had been when he walked home.

Scrooge closed the window, and examined the door by which the Ghost had entered. It was double locked, as he had locked it with his own hands, and the bolts were undisturbed. He tried to say 'Humbug!' but stopped at the first syllable. And being, from the emotions he had undergone, or the fatigues of the day, or his glimpse of the Invisible World, or the dull conversation of the Ghost, or the lateness of the hour, much in need of repose, went straight to bed without undressing, and fell asleep upon the instant.

PART TWO

The First of the Three Spirits

When Scrooge awoke it was so dark, that, looking out of bed, he could scarcely distinguish the transparent window from the opaque walls of his chamber. He was endeavouring to pierce the darkness with his ferret eyes, when the chimes of a neighbouring church struck the four quarters. So he listened for the hour.

To his great astonishment, the heavy bell went on from six to seven, and from seven to eight, and regularly up to twelve; then stopped. Twelve! It was past two when he went to bed. The clock was wrong. An icicle must have got into the works. Twelve!

He touched the spring of his repeater, to correct this most preposterous clock. Its rapid little pulse beat twelve, and stopped.

'Why, it isn't possible,' said Scrooge, 'that I can have slept through a whole day and far into another night. It isn't possible that anything has happened to the sun, and this is twelve at noon!'

The idea being an alarming one, he scrambled out of bed, and groped his way to the window. He was obliged to rub the frost off with the sleeve of his dressing-gown before he could see anything; and could see very little then. All he could make out was, that it was still very foggy and extremely cold, and that there was no noise of people running to and fro, and making a great stir, as there unquestionably would have been if night had beaten off bright day, and taken possession of the world. This was a great relief, because 'Three days after sight of this First of Exchange pay to Mr. Ebenezer Scrooge or his order,' and so forth, would have become a mere United States security if there were no days to count by.

Scrooge went to bed again, and thought, and thought, and thought it over and over, and could make nothing of it. The more he thought, the more perplexed he was; and, the more he endeavoured not to think, the more he thought.

Marley's Ghost bothered him exceedingly. Every time he resolved within himself, after mature inquiry, that it was all a dream, his mind flew back again, like a strong spring released, to its first position, and presented the same problem to be worked all through, 'Was it a dream or not?'

Scrooge lay in this state until the chime had gone three-quarters more, when he remembered, on a sudden, that the Ghost had warned him of a visitation when the bell tolled one. He resolved to lie awake until the hour was passed; and, considering that he could no more go to sleep than go to heaven, this was, perhaps, the wisest resolution in his power.

The quarter was so long, that he was more than once convinced he must have sunk into a doze unconsciously, and missed the clock. At length it broke upon his listening ear.

'Ding, dong!'

'A quarter past,' said Scrooge, counting.

'Ding, dong!'

'Half past,' said Scrooge.

'Ding, dong!'

'A quarter to it,' said Scrooge.

'Ding, dong!'

'The hour itself,' said Scrooge triumphantly, 'and nothing else!'

He spoke before the hour bell sounded, which it now did with a deep, dull, hollow, melancholy ONE. Light flashed up in the room upon the instant, and the curtains of his bed were drawn.

The curtains of his bed were drawn aside, I tell you, by a hand. Not the curtains at his feet, nor the curtains at his back, but those to which his face was addressed. The curtains of his bed were drawn aside; and Scrooge, starting up into a half-recumbent attitude, found himself face to face with the unearthly visitor who drew them: as close to it as I am now to you, and I am standing in the spirit at your elbow.

It was a strange figure—like a child; yet not so like a child as like an old man, viewed through some supernatural medium, which gave him the appearance of having receded from the view, and being diminished to a child's proportions. Its hair, which hung about its neck and down its back, was white, as if with age; and yet the face had not a wrinkle in it, and the tenderest bloom was on the skin. The arms were very long and muscular; the hands the same, as if its hold were of uncommon strength. Its legs and feet, most delicately formed, were, like those upper members, bare. It wore a tunic of the purest white; and round its waist was bound a lustrous belt, the sheen of which was beautiful. It held a branch of fresh green holly in its hand; and, in singular contradiction of that wintry emblem, had its dress trimmed with summer flowers. But the strangest thing about it was, that from the crown of its head there sprang a bright clear jet of light, by which all this was visible; and which was doubtless the occasion of its using, in its duller moments, a great extinguisher for a cap, which it now held under its arm.

Even this, though, when Scrooge looked at it with increasing steadiness, was *not* its strangest quality. For, as its belt sparkled and glittered, now in one part and now in another, and what was light one instant at another time was dark, so the figure itself fluctuated in its distinctness; being now a thing with one arm, now with one leg, now with twenty legs, now a pair of legs without a head, now a head without a body: of which dissolving parts no outline would be visible in the dense gloom wherein they melted away. And, in the very wonder of this, it would be itself again; distinct and clear as ever.

'Are you the Spirit, sir, whose coming was foretold to me?' asked Scrooge.

'I am!'

The voice was soft and gentle. Singularly low, as if, instead of being so close behind him, it were at a distance.

'Who and what are you?' Scrooge demanded.

'I am the Ghost of Christmas Past.'

'Long Past?' inquired Scrooge, observant of its dwarfish stature.

'No. Your past.'

Perhaps Scrooge could not have told anybody why, if anybody could have asked him; but he had a special desire to see the Spirit in his cap, and begged him to be covered.

'What!' exclaimed the Ghost, 'would you so soon put out, with worldly hands, the light I give? Is it not enough that you are one of those whose passions made this cap, and force me through whole trains of years to wear it low upon my brow?'

Scrooge reverently disclaimed all intention to offend or any knowledge of having wilfully 'bonneted' the Spirit at any period of his life. He then made bold to inquire what business brought him there.

'Your welfare!' said the Ghost.

Scrooge expressed himself much obliged, but could not help thinking that a night of unbroken rest would have been more conducive to that end. The Spirit must have heard him thinking, for it said immediately—

'Your reclamation, then. Take heed!'

It put out its strong hand as it spoke, and clasped him gently by the arm.

'Rise! and walk with me!'

It would have been in vain for Scrooge to plead that the weather and the hour were not adapted to pedestrian purposes; that bed was warm, and the thermometer a long way below freezing; that he was clad but lightly in his slippers, dressing-gown, and night-cap; and that he had a cold upon him at that time. The grasp, though gentle as a woman's hand, was not to be resisted. He rose; but, finding that the Spirit made towards the window, clasped its robe in supplication.

'I am a mortal,' Scrooge remonstrated, 'and liable to fall.'

'Bear but a touch of my hand *there*,' said the Spirit, laying it upon his heart, 'and you shall be upheld in more than this!'

As the words were spoken, they passed through the wall, and stood upon an open country road, with fields on either hand. The city had entirely vanished. Not a vestige of it was to be seen. The darkness and the mist had vanished with it, for it was a clear, cold, winter day, with snow upon the ground.

'Good Heaven!' said Scrooge, clasping his hands together, as he looked about him. 'I was bred in this place. I was a boy here!'

The Spirit gazed upon him mildly. Its gentle touch, though it had been light and instantaneous, appeared still present to the old man's sense of feeling. He was conscious of a thousand odours floating in the air, each one connected with a thousand thoughts, and hopes, and joys, and cares long, long forgotten!

'Your lip is trembling,' said the Ghost. 'And what is that upon your cheek?'

Scrooge muttered, with an unusual catching in his voice, that it was a pimple; and begged the Ghost to lead him where he would.

'You recollect the way?' inquired the Spirit.

'Remember it!' cried Scrooge with fervour; 'I could walk it blindfold.'

'Strange to have forgotten it for so many years!' observed the Ghost. 'Let us go on.'

They walked along the road, Scrooge recognising every gate, and post, and tree, until a little market-town appeared in the distance, with its bridge, its church, and winding river. Some shaggy ponies now were seen trotting towards them with boys upon their backs, who called to other boys in country gigs and carts, driven by farmers. All these boys were in great spirits, and shouted to each other, until the broad fields were so full of merry music, that the crisp air laughed to hear it.

'These are but shadows of the things that have been,' said the Ghost. 'They have no consciousness of us.'

The jocund travellers came on; and as they came, Scrooge knew and named them every one. Why was he rejoiced beyond all bounds to see them? Why did his cold eye glisten, and his heart leap up as they went past? Why was he filled with gladness when he heard them give each other Merry Christmas, as they parted at cross-roads and by-ways for their several homes? What was merry Christmas to Scrooge? Out upon merry Christmas! What good had it ever done to him?

'The school is not quite deserted,' said the Ghost. 'A solitary child, neglected by his friends, is left there still.'

Scrooge said he knew it. And he sobbed.

They left the high-road by a well-remembered lane and soon approached a mansion of dull red brick, with a little weather-cock surmounted cupola on the roof, and a bell hanging in it. It was a large house, but one of broken fortunes; for the spacious offices were little used, their walls were damp and mossy, their windows broken, and their gates decayed. Fowls clucked and strutted in the stables; and the coach-houses and sheds were overrun with grass. Nor was it more retentive of its ancient state within; for, entering the dreary hall, and glancing through the open doors of many rooms, they found them poorly furnished, cold, and vast. There was an earthy savour in the air, a chilly bareness in the place, which associated itself somehow with too much getting up by candle light and not too much to eat.

They went, the Ghost and Scrooge, across the hall, to a door at the back of the house. It opened before them, and disclosed a long, bare, melancholy room, made barer still by lines of plain deal forms and desks. At one of these a lonely boy was reading near a feeble fire; and Scrooge sat down upon a form, and wept to see his poor forgotten self as he had used to be.

Not a latent echo in the house, not a squeak and scuffle from the mice behind the panelling, not a drip from the half-thawed waterspout in the dull yard behind, not a sigh among the leafless boughs of one despondent poplar, not the idle swinging of an empty storehouse door, no, not a clicking in the fire, but fell upon the heart of Scrooge with softening influence, and gave a freer passage to his tears.

The Spirit touched him on the arm, and pointed to his younger self, intent upon his reading. Suddenly a man in foreign garments, wonderfully real and distinct to look at, stood outside the window, with an axe stuck in his belt,and leading by the bridle an ass laden with wood.

'Why, it's Ali Baba!' Scrooge exclaimed in ecstasy. 'It's dear old honest Ali Baba! Yes, yes, I know. One Christmas-time, when yonder solitary child was left here all alone, he *did* come, for the first time, just like that. Poor boy! And Valentine,' said Scrooge, 'and his wild brother, Orson; there they go! And what's his name, who was put down in his drawers, asleep, at the gate of Damascus; don't you see him? And the Sultan's Groom turned upside down by the Genii; there he is upon his head! Serve him right! I'm glad of it. What business had he to be married to the Princess?'

To hear Scrooge expending all the earnestness of his nature on such subjects, in a most extraordinary voice between laughing and crying; and to see his heightened and excited face; would have been a surprise to his business friends in the City, indeed.

'There's the Parrot!' cried Scrooge. 'Green body and yellow tail, with a thing like a lettuce growing out of the top of his head; there he is! Poor Robin Crusoe he called him, when he came home again after sailing round the island. "Poor Robin Crusoe, where have you been, Robin Crusoe?" The man thought he was dreaming, but he wasn't. It was the Parrot, you know. There goes Friday, running for his life to the little creek! Halloa! Hoop! Halloo!'

Then, with a rapidity of transition very foreign to his usual character, he said, in pity for his former self, 'Poor boy!' and cried again.

'I wish,' Scrooge muttered, putting his hand in his pocket, and looking about him, after drying his eyes with his cuff; 'but it's too late now.'

'What is the matter?' asked the Spirit.

'Nothing,' said Scrooge. 'Nothing. There was a boy singing a Christmas carol at my door last night. I should like to have given him something: that's all.'

The Ghost smiled thoughtfully, and waved its hand, saying as it did so, 'Let us see another Christmas!'

Scrooge's former self grew larger at the words, and the room became a little darker and more dirty. The panels shrunk, the windows cracked; fragments of plaster fell out of the ceiling, and the naked laths were shown instead; but how all this was brought about Scrooge knew no more than you do. He only knew that it was quite correct; that everything had happened so; that there he was, alone again, when all the other boys had gone home for the jolly holidays.

He was not reading now, but walking up and down despairingly. Scrooge looked at the Ghost, and, with a mournful shaking of his head, glanced anxiously towards the door.

It opened; and a little girl, much younger than the boy, came darting in, and, putting her arms about his neck, and often kissing him, addressed him as her 'dear, dear brother.'

'I have come to bring you home, dear brother!' said the child, clapping her tiny hands, and bending down to laugh. 'To bring you home, home, home!'

'Home, little Fan?' returned the boy.

'Yes!' said the child, brimful of glee. 'Home for good and all. Home for ever and ever. Father is so much kinder than he used to be, that home's like heaven! He spoke so gently to me one dear night when I was going to bed, that I was not afraid to ask him once more if you might come home; and he said Yes, you should; and sent me in a coach to bring you. And you're to be a man!' said the child, opening her eyes; 'and are never to come back here; but first we're to be together all the Christmas long, and have the merriest time in all the world.'

'You are quite a woman, little Fan!' exclaimed the boy.

She clapped her hands and laughed, and tried to touch his head; but, being too little laughed again, and stood on tiptoe to embrace him. Then she began to drag him, in her childish eagerness, towards the door; and he, nothing loath to go, accompanied her.

A terrible voice in the hall cried, 'Bring down Master Scrooge's box, there!' and in the hall appeared the schoolmaster himself who glared on Master Scrooge with a ferocious condescension, and threw him into a dreadful state of mind by shaking hands with him. He then conveyed him and his sister into the veriest old well of a shivering best parlour that ever was seen, where the maps upon the wall, and the celestial and terrestrial globes in the windows, were waxy with cold. Here he produced a decanter of curiously light wine, and a block of curiously heavy cake, and administered instalments of those dainties to the young people; at the same time sending out a meagre servant to offer a glass of 'something' to the postboy, who answered that he thanked the gentleman, but, if it was the same tap as he had tasted before, he had rather not. Master Scrooge's trunk being by this time tied on to the top of the chaise, the children bade the schoolmaster good-bye right willingly; and, getting into it, drove gaily down the garden sweep; the quick wheels dashing the hoar-frost and snow from off the dark leaves of the evergreens like spray.

'Always a delicate creature, whom a breath might have withered,' said the Ghost. 'But she had a large heart!'

'So she had,' cried Scrooge. 'You're right. I will not gainsay it, Spirit. God forbid!'

'She died a woman,' said the Ghost, 'and had, as I think, children.'

'One child,' Scrooge returned.

'True,' said the Ghost. 'Your nephew!'

Scrooge seemed uneasy in his mind, and answered briefly, 'Yes.'

Although they had but that moment left the school behind them, they were now in the busy thoroughfares of a city, where shadowy passengers passed and repassed; where shadowy carts and coaches battled for the way, and all the strife and tumult of a real city were. It was made plain enough, by the dressing of the shops, that here, too, it was Christmas-time again; but it was evening, and the streets were lighted up.

The Ghost stopped at a certain warehouse door, and asked Scrooge if he knew it.

'Know it!' said Scrooge. 'Was I apprenticed here?'

They went in. At sight of an old gentleman in a Welsh wig, sitting behind such a high desk, that if he had been two inches taller, he must have knocked his head against the ceiling, Scrooge cried in great excitement—

'Why, it's old Fezziwig! Bless his heart, it's Fezziwig alive again!'

Old Fezziwig laid down his pen, and looked up at the clock, which pointed to the hour of seven. He rubbed his hands; adjusted his capacious waistcoat; laughed all over himself, from his shoes to his organ of benevolence; and called out, in a comfortable, oily, rich, fat, jovial voice—

'Yo ho, there! Ebenezer! Dick!'

Scrooge's former self, now grown a young man, came briskly in, accompanied by his fellow-'prentice.

'Dick Wilkins, to be sure!' said Scrooge to the Ghost. 'Bless me, yes. There he is. He was very much attached to me, was Dick. Poor Dick! Dear, dear!'

'Yo ho, my boys!' said Fezziwig. 'No more work tonight. Christmas Eve, Dick. Christmas, Ebenezer! Let's have the shutters up,' cried old Fezziwig, with a sharp clap of his hands, 'before a man can say Jack Robinson!'

You wouldn't believe how those two fellows went at it! They charged into the street with the shutters—one, two, three—had 'em up in their places—four, five, six—barred 'em and pinned 'em—seven, eight, nine—and came back before you could have got to twelve, panting like racehorses.

'Hilli-ho!' cried old Fezziwig, skipping down from the high desk with wonderful agility. 'Clear away, my lads, and let's have lots of room here! Hilli-ho, Dick! Chirrup, Ebenezer!'

Clear away! There was nothing they wouldn't have cleared away, or couldn't have cleared away, with old Fezziwig looking on. It was done in a minute. Every movable was packed off, as if it were dismissed from public life for evermore; the floor was swept and watered, the lamps were trimmed, fuel was heaped upon the fire; and the warehouse was as snug, and warm, and dry, and bright a ball-room as you would desire to see upon a winter's night.

In came a fiddler with a music-book, and went up to the lofty desk, and made an orchestra of it, and tuned like fifty stomach-aches. In came Mrs. Fezziwig, one vast substantial smile. In came the three Miss Fezziwigs, beaming and lovable. In came the six young followers whose hearts they broke. In came all the young men and women employed in the business. In came the housemaid, with her cousin the baker. In came the cook with her brother's particular friend the milkman. In came the boy from over the way, who was suspected of not having board enough from his master; trying to hide himself behind the girl from next door but one, who was proved to have had her ears pulled by her mistress. In they all came, one after another; some shyly, some boldly, some gracefully, some awkwardly, some pushing, some pulling; in they all came, any how and every how. Away they all went, twenty couple at once; hands half round and back again the other way; down the middle and up again; round and round in various stages of affectionate grouping; old top couple always turning up in the wrong place; new top couple starting off again as soon as they got there; all top couples at last, and not a bottom one to help them! When this result was brought about, old Fezziwig, clapping his hands to stop the dance, cried out, 'Well done!' and the fiddler plunged his hot face into a pot of porter, especially provided for that purpose. But, scorning rest upon his reappearance, he instantly began again, though there were no dancers yet, as if the other fiddler had been carried home, exhausted, on a shutter, and he were a bran-new man resolved to beat him out of sight, or perish.

There were more dances, and there were forfeits, and more dances, and there was cake, and there was negus, and there was a great piece of Cold Roast, and there was a great piece of Cold Boiled, and there were mince-pies, and plenty of beer. But the great effect of the evening came after the Roast and Boiled, when the fiddler (an artful dog, mind! The sort of man who knew his business better than you or I could have told it him!) struck up 'Sir Roger de Coverley.' Then old Fezziwig stood out to dance with Mrs. Fezziwig. Top couple, too; with a good stiff piece of work cut out for them; three or four and twenty pair of partners; people who were not to be trifled with; people who would dance, and bad no notion of walking.

But if they had been twice as many—ah! four times—old Fezziwig would have been a match for them, and so would Mrs. Fezziwig. As to *her*, she was worthy to be his partner in every sense of the term. If that's not high praise, tell me higher, and I'll use it. A positive light appeared to issue from Fezziwig's calves. They shone in every part of the dance like moons. You couldn't have predicted, at any given time, what would become of them next. And when old Fezziwig and Mrs. Fezziwig had gone all through the dance; advance and retire, both hands to your partner, bow and curtsy, cork-screw, thread-the-needle, and back again to your place: Fezziwig 'cut'—cut so deftly, that he appeared to wink with his legs, and came upon his feet again without a stagger.

When the clock struck eleven, this domestic ball broke up. Mr. and Mrs. Fezziwig took their stations, one on either side the door, and, shaking hands with every person individually as he or she went out, wished him or her a Merry Christmas. When everybody had retired but the two 'prentices, they did the same to them; and thus the cheerful voices died away, and the lads were left to their beds; which were under a counter in the back-shop.

During the whole of this time Scrooge had acted like a man out of his wits. His heart and soul were in the scene, and with his former self. He corroborated everything, remembered everything, enjoyed everything, and underwent the strangest agitation. It was not until now, when the bright faces of his former self and Dick were turned from them, that he remembered the Ghost, and became conscious that it was looking full upon him, while the light upon its head burnt very clear.

'A small matter,' said the Ghost, 'to make these silly folks so full of gratitude.'

'Small!' echoed Scrooge.

The Spirit signed to him to listen to the two apprentices, who were pouring out their hearts in praise of Fezziwig; and when he had done so, said:

'Why! Is it not? He has spent but a few pounds of your mortal money: three or four, perhaps. Is that so much that he deserves this praise?'

'It isn't that,' said Scrooge, heated by the remark, and speaking unconsciously like his former, not his latter self. 'It isn't that, Spirit. He has the power to render us happy or unhappy; to make our service light or burdensome; a pleasure or a toil. Say that his power lies in words and looks; in things so slight and insignificant that it is impossible to add and count 'em up: what then? The happiness he gives is quite as great as if it cost a fortune.'

He felt the Spirit's glance, and stopped.

'What is the matter?' asked the Ghost.

'Nothing particular,' said Scrooge.

'Something, I think?' the Ghost insisted.

'No,' said Scrooge, 'no. I should like to be able to say a word or two to my clerk just now. That's all.'

His former self turned down the lamps as he gave utterance to the wish; and Scrooge and the Ghost again stood side by side in the open air.

'My time grows short,' observed the Spirit. 'Quick!'

This was not addressed to Scrooge, or to any one whom he could see, but it produced an immediate effect. For again Scrooge saw himself. He was older now; a man in the prime of life. His face had not the harsh and rigid lines of later years; but it had begun to wear the signs of care and avarice. There was an eager, greedy, restless motion in the eye, which showed the passion that had taken root, and where the shadow of the growing tree would fall.

He was not alone, but sat by the side of a fair young girl in a mourning dress: in whose eyes there were tears, which sparkled in the light that shone out of the Ghost of Christmas Past.

'It matters little,' she said softly. 'To you, very little. Another idol has displaced me; and, if it can cheer and comfort you in time to come as I would have tried to do, I have no just cause to grieve.'

'What Idol has displaced you?' he rejoined.

'A golden one.'

'This is the even-handed dealing of the world!' he said. 'There is nothing on which it is so hard as poverty; and there is nothing it professes to condemn with such severity as the pursuit of wealth!'

'You fear the world too much,' she answered gently. 'All your other hopes have merged into the hope of being beyond the chance of its sordid reproach. I have seen your nobler aspirations fall off one by one, until the master passion, Gain, engrosses you. Have I not?'

'What then?' he retorted. 'Even if I have grown so much wiser, what then? I am not changed towards you.'

She shook her head.

'Am I?'

'Our contract is an old one. It was made when we were both poor, and content to be so, until, in good season, we could improve our worldly fortune by our patient industry. You *are* changed. When it was made you were another man.'

'I was a boy,' he said impatiently.

'Your own feeling tells you that you were not what you are,' she returned. 'I am. That which promised happiness when we were one in heart is fraught with misery now that we are two. How often and how keenly I have thought of this I will not say. It is enough that I *have* thought of it, and can release you.'

'Have I ever sought release?'

'In words. No. Never.'

'In what, then?'

'In a changed nature; in an altered spirit; in another atmosphere of life; another Hope as its great end. In everything that made my love of any worth or value in your sight. If this had never been between us,' said the girl, looking mildly, but with steadiness, upon him; 'tell me, would you seek me out and try to win me now? Ah, no!'

He seemed to yield to the justice of this supposition in spite of himself. But he said, with a struggle, 'You think not.'

'I would gladly think otherwise if I could,' she answered. 'Heaven knows! When *I* have learned a Truth like this, I know how strong and irresistible it must be. But if you were free today, tomorrow, yesterday, can even I believe that you would choose a dowerless girl—you who, in your very confidence with her, weigh everything by Gain: or, choosing her, if for a moment you were false enough to your one guiding principle to do so, do I not know that your repentance and regret would surely follow? I do; and I release you. With a full heart, for the love of him you once were.'

He was about to speak; but, with her head turned from him, she resumed:

'You may—the memory of what is past half makes me hope you will—have pain in this. A very, very brief time, and you will dismiss the recollection of it gladly, as an unprofitable dream, from which it happened well that you awoke. May you be happy in the life you have chosen!'

She left him, and they parted.

'Spirit!' said Scrooge, 'show me no more! Conduct me home. Why do you delight to torture me?'

'One shadow more!' exclaimed the Ghost.

'No more!' cried Scrooge. 'No more! I don't wish to see it. Show me no more!'

But the relentless Ghost pinioned him in both his arms, and forced him to observe what happened next.

They were in another scene and place; a room, not very large or handsome, but full of comfort. Near to the winter fire sat a beautiful young girl, so like that last that Scrooge believed it was the same, until he saw *her*, now a comely matron, sitting opposite her daughter. The noise in this room was perfectly tumultuous, for there were more children there than Scrooge in his agitated state of mind could count; and, unlike the celebrated herd in the poem, they were not forty children conducting themselves like one, but every child was conducting itself like forty. The consequences were uproarious beyond belief; but no one seemed to care; on the contrary, the mother and daughter laughed heartily, and enjoyed it very much; and the latter, soon beginning to mingle in the sports, got pillaged by the young brigands most ruthlessly. What would I not have given to be one of them! Though I never could have been so rude, no, no! I wouldn't for the wealth of all the world have crushed that braided hair, and torn it down; and for the precious little shoe, I wouldn't have plucked it off, God bless my soul! to save my life. As to measuring her waist in sport, as they did, bold young brood, I couldn't have done it; I should have expected my arm to have grown round it for a punishment, and never come straight again. And yet I should have dearly liked, I own, to have touched her lips; to have questioned her, that she might have opened them; to have looked upon the lashes of her downcast eyes, and never raised a blush; to have let loose waves of hair, an inch of which would be a keepsake beyond price: in short, I should have liked, I do confess, to have had the lightest licence of a child, and yet to have been man enough to know its value.

But now a knocking at the door was heard, and such a rush immediately ensued that she, with laughing face and plundered dress, was borne towards it the centre of a flushed and boisterous group, just in time to greet the father, who came home attended by a man laden with Christmas toys and presents. Then the shouting and the struggling, and the onslaught that was made on the defenceless porter! The scaling him, with chairs for ladders, to dive into his pockets, despoil him of brown-paper parcels, hold on tight by his cravat, hug him round his neck, pummel his back, and kick his legs in irrepressible affection! The shouts of wonder and delight with which the development of every package was received! The terrible announcement that the baby had been taken in the act of putting a doll's frying pan into his mouth, and was more than suspected of having swallowed a fictitious turkey, glued on a wooden platter! The immense relief of finding this a false alarm! The joy, and gratitude, and ecstasy! They are all indescribable alike. It is enough that, by degrees, the children and their emotions got out of the parlour, and, by one stair at a time, up to the top of the house, where they went to bed, and so subsided.

And now Scrooge looked on more attentively than ever, when the master of the house, having his daughter leaning fondly on him, sat down with her and her mother at his own fireside; and when he thought that such another creature, quite as graceful and as full of promise, might have called him father, and been a spring-time in the haggard winter of his life, his sight grew very dim indeed.

'Belle,' said the husband, turning to his wife with a smile, 'I saw an old friend of yours this afternoon.'

'Who was it?'

'Guess!'

'How can I? Tut, don't I know?' she added in the same breath, laughing as he laughed. 'Mr. Scrooge.'

'Mr. Scrooge it was. I passed his office window; and as it was not shut up, and he had a candle inside, I could scarcely help seeing him. His partner lies upon the point of death, I hear; and there he sat alone. Quite alone in the world, I do believe.'

'Spirit!' said Scrooge in a broken voice, 'remove me from this place.'

'I told you these were shadows of the things that have been,' said the Ghost. 'That they are what they are do not blame me!'

'Remove me!' Scrooge exclaimed, 'I cannot bear it!'

He turned upon the Ghost, and seeing that it looked upon him with a face, in which in some strange way there were fragments of all the faces it had shown him, wrestled with it.

'Leave me! Take me back. Haunt me no longer!'

In the struggle, if that can be called a struggle in which the Ghost with no visible resistance on its own part was undisturbed by any effort of its adversary, Scrooge observed that its light was burning high and bright; and dimly connecting that with its influence over him, he seized the extinguisher-cap, and by a sudden action pressed it down upon its head.

The Spirit dropped beneath it, so that the extinguisher covered its whole form; but though Scrooge pressed it down with all his force, he could not hide the light, which streamed from under it, in an unbroken flood upon the ground.

He was conscious of being exhausted, and overcome by an irresistible drowsiness; and, further, of being in his own bedroom. He gave the cap a parting squeeze, in which his hand relaxed; and had barely time to reel to bed, before he sank into a heavy sleep.

PART THREE

The Second of the Three Spirits

Awaking in the middle of a prodigiously tough snore, and sitting up in bed to get his thoughts together, Scrooge had no occasion to be told that the bell was again upon the stroke of One. He felt that he was restored to consciousness in the right nick of time, for the especial purpose of holding a conference with the second messenger despatched to him through Jacob Marley's intervention. But finding that he turned uncomfortably cold when he began to wonder which of his curtains this new spectre would draw back, he put them every one aside with his own hands, and, lying down again, established a sharp look-out all round the bed. For he wished to challenge the Spirit on the moment of its appearance, and did not wish to be taken by surprise and made nervous.

Gentlemen of the free-and-easy sort, who plume themselves on being acquainted with a move or two, and being usually equal to the time of day, express the wide range of their capacity for adventure by observing that they are good for anything from pitch-and-toss to manslaughter; between which opposite extremes, no doubt, there lies a tolerably wide and comprehensive range of subjects. Without venturing for Scrooge quite as hardily as this, I don't mind calling on you to believe that he was ready for a good broad field of strange appearances, and that nothing between a baby and a rhinoceros would have astonished him very much.

Now, being prepared for almost anything, he was not by any means prepared for nothing; and consequently, when the bell struck One, and no shape appeared, he was taken with a violent fit of trembling. Five minutes, ten minutes, a quarter of an hour went by, yet nothing came. All this time he lay upon his bed, the very core and centre of a blaze of ruddy light, which streamed upon it when the clock proclaimed the hour; and which, being only light, was more alarming than a dozen ghosts, as he was powerless to make out what it meant, or would be at; and was sometimes apprehensive that he might be at that very moment an interesting case of spontaneous combustion, without having the consolation of knowing it. At last, however, he began to think—as you or I would have thought at first; for it is always the person not in the predicament who knows what ought to have been done in it, and would unquestionably have done it too—at last, I say, he began to think that the source and secret of this ghostly light might be in the adjoining room, from whence, on further tracing it, it seemed to shine. This idea taking full possession of his mind, he got up softly, and shuffled in his slippers to the door.

The moment Scrooge's hand was on the lock a strange voice called him by his name, and bade him enter. He obeyed.

It was his own room. There was no doubt about that. But it had undergone a surprising transformation. The walls and ceiling were so hung with living green, that it looked a perfect grove; from every part of which bright gleaming berries glistened. The crisp leaves of holly, mistletoe, and ivy reflected back the light, as if so many little mirrors had been scattered there; and such a mighty blaze went roaring up the chimney as that dull petrification of a hearth had never known in Scrooge's time, or Marley's, or for many and many a winter season gone. Heaped up on the floor, to form a kind of throne, were turkeys, geese, game, poultry, brawn, great joints of meat, sucking-pigs, long wreaths of sausages, mince-pies, plum-puddings, barrels of oysters, red-hot chestnuts, cherry-cheeked apples, juicy oranges, luscious pears, immense twelfth-cakes, and seething bowls of punch, that made the chamber dim with their delicious steam. In easy state upon this couch there sat a jolly Giant, glorious to see; who bore a glowing torch, in shape not unlike Plenty's horn, and held it up, high up, to shed its light on Scrooge as he came peeping round the door.

'Come in!' exclaimed the Ghost. 'Come in! and know me better, man!'

Scrooge entered timidly, and hung his head before this Spirit. He was not the dogged Scrooge he had been; and though the Spirit's eyes were clear and kind, he did not like to meet them.

'I am the Ghost of Christmas Present,' said the Spirit. 'Look upon me!'

Scrooge reverently did so. It was clothed in one simple deep green robe, or mantle, bordered with white fur. This garment hung so loosely on the figure, that its capacious breast was bare, as if disdaining to be warded or concealed by any artifice. Its feet, observable beneath the ample folds of the garment, were also bare; and on its head it wore no other covering than a holly wreath, set here and there with shining icicles. Its dark-brown curls were long and free; free as its genial face, its sparkling eye, its open hand, its cheery voice, its unconstrained demeanour, and its joyful air. Girded round its middle was an antique scabbard; but no sword was in it, and the ancient sheath was eaten up with rust.

'You have never seen the like of me before!' exclaimed the Spirit.

'Never,' Scrooge made answer to it.

'Have never walked forth with the younger members of my family; meaning (for I am very young) my elder brothers born in these later years?' pursued the Phantom.

'I don't think I have,' said Scrooge. 'I am afraid I have not. Have you had many brothers, Spirit?'

'More than eighteen hundred,' said the Ghost.

'A tremendous family to provide for,' muttered Scrooge.

The Ghost of Christmas Present rose.

'Spirit,' said Scrooge submissively, 'conduct me where you will. I went forth last night on compulsion, and I learned a lesson which is working now. Tonight if you have aught to teach me, let me profit by it.'

'Touch my robe!'

Scrooge did as he was told, and held it fast.

Holly, mistletoe, red berries, ivy, turkeys, geese, game, poultry, brawn, meat, pigs, sausages, oysters, pies, puddings, fruit, and punch, all vanished instantly. So did the room, the fire, the ruddy glow, the hour of night, and they stood in the city streets on Christmas morning, where (for the weather was severe) the people made a rough, but brisk and not unpleasant kind of music, in scraping the snow from the pavement in front of their dwellings, and from the tops of their houses, whence it was mad delight to the boys to see it come plumping down into the road below, and splitting into artificial little snowstorms.

The house-fronts looked black enough, and the windows blacker, contrasting with the smooth white sheet of snow upon the roofs, and with the dirtier snow upon the ground; which last deposit had been ploughed up in deep furrows by the heavy wheels of carts and waggons: furrows that crossed and recrossed each other hundreds of times where the great streets branched off; and made intricate channels, hard to trace in the thick yellow mud and icy water. The sky was gloomy, and the shortest streets were choked up with a dingy mist, half thawed, half frozen, whose heavier particles descended in a shower of sooty atoms, as if all the chimneys in Great Britain had, by one consent, caught fire, and were blazing away to their dear heart's content. There was nothing very cheerful in the climate or the town, and yet was there an air of cheerfulness abroad that the clearest summer air and brightest summer sun might have endeavoured to diffuse in vain.

For the people who were shovelling away on the house-tops were jovial and full of glee; calling out to one another from the parapets, and now and then exchanging a facetious snowball—better-natured missile far than many a wordy jest—laughing heartily if it went right, and not less heartily if it went wrong. The poulterers' shops were still half open, and the fruiterers' were radiant in their glory. There were great, round, pot-bellied baskets of chestnuts, shaped like the waistcoats of jolly old gentlemen, lolling at the doors, and tumbling out into the street in their apoplectic opulence: There were ruddy, brown-faced, broad-girthed Spanish onions, shining in the fatness of their growth like Spanish friars, and winking from their shelves in wanton slyness at the girls as they went by, and glanced demurely at the hung-up mistletoe. There were pears and apples clustered high in blooming pyramids; there were bunches of grapes, made, in the shopkeepers' benevolence, to dangle from conspicuous hooks that people's mouths might water gratis as they passed; there were piles of filberts, mossy and brown, recalling, in their fragrance, ancient walks among the woods, and pleasant shufflings ankle deep through withered leaves; there were Norfolk Biffins, squab and swarthy, setting off the yellow of the oranges and lemons, and, in the great compactness of their juicy persons, urgently entreating and beseeching to be carried home in paper bags and eaten after dinner. The very gold and silver fish, set forth among these choice fruits in a bowl, though members of a dull and stagnant-blooded race, appeared to know that there was something going on; and, to a fish, went gasping round and round their little world in slow and passionless excitement.

The Grocers'! oh, the Grocers'! nearly closed, with perhaps two shutters down, or one; but through those gaps such glimpses! It was not alone that the scales descending on the counter made a merry sound, or that the twine and roller parted company so briskly, or that the canisters were rattled up and down like juggling tricks, or even that the blended scents of tea and coffee were so grateful to the nose, or even that the raisins were so plentiful and rare, the almonds so extremely white, the sticks of cinnamon so long and straight, the other spices so delicious, the candied fruits so caked and spotted with molten sugar as to make the coldest lookers-on feel faint, and subsequently bilious. Nor was it that the figs were moist and pulpy, or that the French plums blushed in modest tartness from their highly decorated boxes, or that everything was good to eat and in its Christmas dress; but the customers were all so hurried and so eager in the hopeful promise of the day, that they tumbled up against each other at the door, crashing their wicker baskets wildly, and left their purchases upon the counter, and came running back to fetch them, and committed hundreds of the like mistakes, in the best humour possible; while the grocer and his people were so frank and fresh, that the polished hearts with which they fastened their aprons behind might have been their own, worn outside for general inspection, and for Christmas daws to peck at if they chose.

But soon the steeples called good people all to church and chapel, and away they came, flocking through the streets in their best clothes and with their gayest faces. And at the same time there emerged, from scores of by-streets, lanes, and nameless turnings, innumerable people, carrying their dinners to the bakers' shops. The sight of these poor revellers appeared to interest the Spirit very much, for he stood with Scrooge beside him in a baker's doorway, and, taking off the covers as their bearers passed, sprinkled incense on their dinners from his torch. And it was a very uncommon kind of torch, for once or twice, when there were angry words between some dinner-carriers who had jostled each other, he shed a few drops of water on them from it, and their good-humour was restored directly. For they said, it was a shame to quarrel upon Christmas Day. And so it was! God love it, so it was!

In time the bells ceased, and the bakers were shut up; and yet there was a genial shadowing forth of all these dinners, and the progress of their cooking, in the thawed blotch of wet above each baker's oven, where the pavement smoked as if its stones were cooking too.

'Is there a peculiar flavour in what you sprinkle from your torch?' asked Scrooge.

'There is. My own.'

'Would it apply to any kind of dinner on this day?' asked Scrooge.

'To any kindly given. To a poor one most.'

'Why to a poor one most?' asked Scrooge.

'Because it needs it most.'

'Spirit!' said Scrooge, after a moment's thought, 'I wonder you, of all the beings in the many worlds about us, should desire to cramp these people's opportunities of innocent enjoyment.'

'I!' cried the Spirit.

'You would deprive them of their means of dining every seventh day, often the only day on which they can be said to dine at all,' said Scrooge; 'wouldn't you?'

'I!' cried the Spirit.

'You seek to close these places on the Seventh Day,' said Scrooge. 'And it comes to the same thing.'

'I seek!' exclaimed the Spirit.

'Forgive me if I am wrong. It has been done in your name, or at least in that of your family,' said Scrooge.

'There are some upon this earth of yours,' returned the Spirit, 'who lay claim to know us, and who do their deeds of passion, pride, ill-will, hatred, envy, bigotry, and selfishness in our name, who are as strange to us, and all our kith and kin, as if they had never lived. Remember that, and charge their doings on themselves, not us.'

Scrooge promised that he would; and they went on, invisible, as they had been before, into the suburbs of the town. It was a remarkable quality of the Ghost (which Scrooge had observed at the baker's), that notwithstanding his gigantic size, he could accommodate himself to any place with ease; and that he stood beneath a low roof quite as gracefully and like a supernatural creature as it was possible he could have done in any lofty hall.

And perhaps it was the pleasure the good Spirit had in showing off this power of his, or else it was his own kind, generous, hearty nature, and his sympathy with all poor men, that led him straight to Scrooge's clerk's; for there he went, and took Scrooge with him, holding to his robe; and on the threshold of the door the Spirit smiled, and stopped to bless Bob Cratchit's dwelling with the sprinklings of his torch. Think of that! Bob had but fifteen 'Bob' a week himself; he pocketed on Saturdays but fifteen copies of his Christian name; and yet the Ghost of Christmas Present blessed his four-roomed house!

Then up rose Mrs. Cratchit, Cratchit's wife, dressed out but poorly in a twice-turned gown, but brave in ribbons, which are cheap, and make a goodly show for sixpence; and she laid the cloth, assisted by Belinda Cratchit, second of her daughters, also brave in ribbons; while Master Peter Cratchit plunged a fork into the saucepan of potatoes, and getting the corners of his monstrous shirt-collar (Bob's private property, conferred upon his son and heir in honour of the day, into his mouth, rejoiced to find himself so gallantly attired, and yearned to show his linen in the fashionable Parks. And now two smaller Cratchits, boy and girl, came tearing in, screaming that outside the baker's they had smelt the goose, and known it for their own; and basking in luxurious thoughts of sage and onion, these young Cratchits danced about the table, and exalted Master Peter Cratchit to the skies, while he (not proud, although his collars nearly choked him) blew the fire, until the slow potatoes, bubbling up, knocked loudly at the saucepan-lid to be let out and peeled.

'What has ever got your precious father, then?' said Mrs. Cratchit. 'And your brother, Tiny Tim? And Martha warn't as late last Christmas Day by half an hour!'

'Here's Martha, mother!' said a girl, appearing as she spoke.

'Here's Martha, mother!' cried the two young Cratchits. 'Hurrah! There's *such* a goose, Martha!'

'Why, bless your heart alive, my dear, how late you are!' said Mrs. Cratchit, kissing her a dozen times, and taking off her shawl and bonnet for her with officious zeal.

'We'd a deal of work to finish up last night,' replied the girl, 'and had to clear away this morning, mother!'

'Well! never mind so long as you are come,' said Mrs. Cratchit. 'Sit ye down before the fire, my dear, and have a warm, Lord bless ye!'

'No, no! There's father coming,' cried the two young Cratchits, who were everywhere at once. 'Hide, Martha, hide!'

So Martha hid herself, and in came little Bob, the father, with at least three feet of comforter, exclusive of the fringe, hanging down before him, and his threadbare clothes darned up and brushed to look seasonable, and Tiny Tim upon his shoulder. Alas for Tiny Tim, he bore a little crutch, and had his limbs supported by an iron frame!

'Why, where's our Martha?' cried Bob Cratchit, looking round.

'Not coming,' said Mrs. Cratchit.

'Not coming!' said Bob, with a sudden declension in his high spirits; for he had been Tim's blood-horse all the way from church, and had come home rampant. 'Not coming upon Christmas Day!'

Martha didn't like to see him disappointed, if it were only in joke; so she came out prematurely from behind the closet door, and ran into his arms, while the two young Cratchits hustled Tiny Tim, and bore him off into the wash-house, that he might hear the pudding singing in the copper.

'And how did little Tim behave?' asked Mrs. Cratchit when she had rallied Bob on his credulity, and Bob had hugged his daughter to his heart's content.

'As good as gold,' said Bob, 'and better. Somehow, he gets thoughtful, sitting by himself so much, and thinks the strangest things you ever heard. He told me, coming home, that he hoped the people saw him in the church, because he was a cripple, and it might be pleasant to them to remember upon Christmas Day who made lame beggars walk and blind men see.'

Bob's voice was tremulous when he told them this, and trembled more when he said that Tiny Tim was growing strong and hearty.

His active little crutch was heard upon the floor, and back came Tiny Tim before another word was spoken, escorted by his brother and sister to his stool beside the fire; and while Bob, turning up his cuffs—as if, poor fellow, they were capable of being made more shabby—compounded some hot mixture in a jug with gin and lemons, and stirred it round and round, and put it on the hob to simmer, Master Peter and the two ubiquitous young Cratchits went to fetch the goose, with which they soon returned in high procession.

Such a bustle ensued that you might have thought a goose the rarest of all birds; a feathered phenomenon, to which a black swan was a matter of course—and, in truth, it was something very like it in that house. Mrs. Cratchit made the gravy (ready beforehand in a little saucepan) hissing hot; Master Peter mashed the potatoes with incredible vigour; Miss Belinda sweetened up the apple sauce; Martha dusted the hot plates; Bob took Tiny Tim beside him in a tiny corner at the table; the two young Cratchits set chairs for everybody, not forgetting themselves, and, mounting guard upon their posts, crammed spoons into their mouths, lest they should shriek for goose before their turn came to be helped. At last the dishes were set on, and grace was said. It was succeeded by a breathless pause, as Mrs. Cratchit, looking slowly all along the carving-knife, prepared to plunge it in the breast; but when she did, and when the long-expected gush of stuffing issued forth, one murmur of delight arose all round the board, and even Tiny Tim, excited by the two young Cratchits, beat on the table with the handle of his knife and feebly cried Hurrah!

There never was such a goose. Bob said he didn't believe there ever was such a goose cooked. Its tenderness and flavour, size and cheapness, were the themes of universal admiration. Eked out by apple sauce and mashed potatoes, it was a sufficient dinner for the whole family; indeed, as Mrs. Cratchit said with great delight (surveying one small atom of a bone upon the dish), they hadn't ate it all at last! Yet every one had had enough, and the youngest Cratchits, in particular, were steeped in sage and onion to the eyebrows! But now, the plates being changed by Miss Belinda, Mrs. Cratchit left the room alone—too nervous to bear witnesses—to take the pudding up, and bring it in.

Suppose it should not be done enough! Suppose it should break in turning out! Suppose somebody should have got over the wall of the back-yard and stolen it, while they were merry with the goose—a supposition at which the two young Cratchits became livid! All sorts of horrors were supposed.

Hallo! A great deal of steam! The pudding was out of the copper. A smell like a washing-day! That was the cloth. A smell like an eating-house and a pastry-cook's next door to each other, with a laundress's next door to that! That was the pudding! In half a minute Mrs. Cratchit entered—flushed, but smiling proudly—with the pudding, like a speckled cannon-ball, so hard and firm, blazing in half of half-a-quarter of ignited brandy, and bedight with Christmas holly stuck into the top.

Oh, a wonderful pudding! Bob Cratchit said, and calmly too, that he regarded it as the greatest success achieved by Mrs. Cratchit since their marriage. Mrs. Cratchit said that, now the weight was off her mind, she would confess she had her doubts about the quantity of flour. Everybody had something to say about it, but nobody said or thought it was at all a small pudding for a large family. It would have been flat heresy to do so. Any Cratchit would have blushed to hint at such a thing.

At last the dinner was all done, the cloth was cleared, the hearth swept, and the fire made up. The compound in the jug being tasted, and considered perfect, apples and oranges were put upon the table, and a shovel full of chestnuts on the fire. Then all the Cratchit family drew round the hearth in what Bob Cratchit called a circle, meaning half a one; and at Bob Cratchit's elbow stood the family display of glass. Two tumblers and a custard cup without a handle.

These held the hot stuff from the jug, however, as well as golden goblets would have done; and Bob served it out with beaming looks, while the chestnuts on the fire sputtered and cracked noisily. Then Bob proposed:

'A merry Christmas to us all, my dears. God bless us!'

Which all the family re-echoed.

'God bless us every one!' said Tiny Tim, the last of all.

He sat very close to his father's side, upon his little stool. Bob held his withered little hand to his, as if he loved the child, and wished to keep him by his side, and dreaded that he might be taken from him.

'Spirit,' said Scrooge, with an interest he had never felt before, 'tell me if Tiny Tim will live.'

'I see a vacant seat,' replied the Ghost, 'in the poor chimney corner, and a crutch without an owner, carefully preserved. If these shadows remain unaltered by the Future, the child will die.'

'No, no,' said Scrooge. 'Oh no, kind Spirit! say he will be spared.'

'If these shadows remain unaltered by the Future none other of my race,' returned the Ghost, 'will find him here. What then? If he be like to die, he had better do it, and decrease the surplus population.'

Scrooge hung his head to hear his own words quoted by the Spirit, and was overcome with penitence and grief.

'Man,' said the Ghost, 'if man you be in heart, not adamant, forbear that wicked cant until you have discovered what the surplus is, and where it is. Will you decide what men shall live, what men shall die? It may be that, in the sight of Heaven, you are more worthless and less fit to live than millions like this poor man's child. O God! to hear the insect on the leaf pronouncing on the too much life among his hungry brothers in the dust!'

Scrooge bent before the Ghost's rebuke, and, trembling, cast his eyes upon the ground. But he raised them speedily on hearing his own name.

'Mr. Scrooge!' said Bob. 'I'll give you Mr. Scrooge, the Founder of the Feast!'

'The Founder of the Feast, indeed!' cried Mrs. Cratchit, reddening. 'I wish I had him here. I'd give him a piece of my mind to feast upon, and I hope he'd have a good appetite for it.'

'My dear,' said Bob,' the children! Christmas Day.'

'It should be Christmas Day, I am sure,' said she, 'on which one drinks the health of such an odious, stingy, hard, unfeeling man as Mr. Scrooge. You know he is, Robert! Nobody knows it better than you do, poor fellow!'

'My dear!' was Bob's mild answer. 'Christmas Day.'

'I'll drink his health for your sake and the Day's,' said Mrs. Cratchit, 'not for his. Long life to him! A merry Christmas and a happy New Year! He'll be very merry and very happy, I have no doubt!'

The children drank the toast after her. It was the first of their proceedings which had no heartiness in it. Tiny Tim drank it last of all, but he didn't care twopence for it. Scrooge was the Ogre of the family. The mention of his name cast a dark shadow on the party, which was not dispelled for full five minutes.

After it had passed away they were ten times merrier than before, from the mere relief of Scrooge the Baleful being done with. Bob Cratchit told them how he had a situation in his eye for Master Peter, which would bring in, if obtained, full five-and-sixpence weekly. The two young Cratchits laughed tremendously at the idea of Peter's being a man of business; and Peter himself looked thoughtfully at the fire from between his collars, as if he were deliberating what particular investments he should favour when he came into the receipt of that bewildering income. Martha, who was a poor apprentice at a milliner's, then told them what kind of work she had to do, and how many hours she worked at a stretch and how she meant to lie abed tomorrow morning for a good long rest; tomorrow being a holiday she passed at home. Also how she had seen a countess and a lord some days before, and how the lord 'was much about as tall as Peter'; at which Peter pulled up his collar so high that you couldn't have seen his head if you had been there. All this time the chestnuts and the jug went round and round; and by-and-by they had a song, about a lost child travelling in the snow, from Tiny Tim, who had a plaintive little voice, and sang it very well indeed.

There was nothing of high mark in this. They were not a handsome family; they were not well dressed; their shoes were far from being waterproof; their clothes were scanty; and Peter might have known, and very likely did, the inside of a pawnbroker's. But they were happy, grateful, pleased with one another, and contented with the time; and when they faded, and looked happier yet in the bright sprinklings of the Spirit's torch at parting, Scrooge had his eye upon them, and especially on Tiny Tim, until the last.

By this time it was getting dark, and snowing pretty heavily; and as Scrooge and the Spirit went along the streets, the brightness of the roaring fires in kitchens, parlours, and all sorts of rooms was wonderful. Here, the flickering of the blaze showed preparations for a cosy dinner, with hot plates baking through and through before the fire, and deep red curtains, ready to be drawn to shut out cold and darkness. There, all the children of the house were running out into the snow to meet their married sisters, brothers, cousins, uncles, aunts, and be the first to greet them. Here, again, were shadows on the window-blinds of guests assembling; and there a group of handsome girls, all hooded and fur-booted, and all chattering at once, tripped lightly off to some near neighbour's house; where, woe upon the single man who saw them enter—artful witches, well they knew it—in a glow!

But, if you had judged from the numbers of people on their way to friendly gatherings, you might have thought that no one was at home to give them welcome when they got there, instead of every house expecting company, and piling up its fires half-chimney high. Blessings on it, how the Ghost exulted! How it bared its breadth of breast, and opened its capacious palm, and floated on, outpouring with a generous hand its bright and harmless mirth on everything within its reach! The very lamplighter, who ran on before, dotting the dusky street with specks of light, and who was dressed to spend the evening somewhere, laughed out loudly as the Spirit passed, though little kenned the lamplighter that he had any company but Christmas.

And now, without a word of warning from the Ghost, they stood upon a bleak and desert moor, where monstrous masses of rude stone were cast about, as though it were the burial-place of giants; and water spread itself wheresoever it listed; or would have done so, but for the frost that held it prisoner; and nothing grew but moss and furze, and coarse, rank grass. Down in the west the setting sun had left a streak of fiery red, which glared upon the desolation for an instant, like a sullen eye, and frowning lower, lower, lower yet, was lost in the thick gloom of darkest night.

'What place is this?' asked Scrooge.

'A place where miners live, who labour in the bowels of the earth,' returned the Spirit. 'But they know me. See!'

A light shone from the window of a hut, and swiftly they advanced towards it. Passing through the wall of mud and stone, they found a cheerful company assembled round a glowing fire. An old, old man and woman, with their children and their children's children, and another generation beyond that, all decked out gaily in their holiday attire. The old man, in a voice that seldom rose above the howling of the wind upon the barren waste, was singing them a Christmas song; it had been a very old song when he was a boy; and from time to time they all joined in the chorus. So surely as they raised their voices, the old man got quite blithe and loud; and so surely as they stopped, his vigour sank again.

The Spirit did not tarry here, but bade Scrooge hold his robe, and, passing on above the moor, sped whither? Not to sea? To sea. To Scrooge's horror, looking back, he saw the last of the land, a frightful range of rocks, behind them; and his ears were deafened by the thundering of water, as it rolled and roared, and raged among the dreadful caverns it had worn, and fiercely tried to undermine the earth.

Built upon a dismal reef of sunken rocks, some league or so from shore, on which the waters chafed and dashed, the wild year through, there stood a solitary lighthouse. Great heaps of seaweed clung to its base, and storm-birds—born of the wind, one might suppose, as seaweed of the water—rose and fell about it, like the waves they skimmed.

But, even here, two men who watched the light had made a fire, that through the loophole in the thick stone wall shed out a ray of brightness on the awful sea. Joining their horny hands over the rough table at which they sat, they wished each other Merry Christmas in their can of grog; and one of them—the elder too, with his face all damaged and scarred with hard weather, as the figure-head of an old ship might be—struck up a sturdy song that was like a gale in itself.

Again the Ghost sped on, above the black and heaving sea—on, on—until being far away, as he told Scrooge, from any shore, they lighted on a ship. They stood beside the helmsman at the wheel, the look-out in the bow, the officers who had the watch; dark, ghostly figures in their several stations; but every man among them hummed a Christmas tune, or had a Christmas thought, or spoke below his breath to his companion of some bygone Christmas Day, with homeward hopes belonging to it. And every man on board, waking or sleeping, good or bad, had had a kinder word for one another on that day than on any day in the year; and had shared to some extent in its festivities; and had remembered those he cared for at a distance, and had known that they delighted to remember him.

It was a great surprise to Scrooge, while listening to the moaning of the wind, and thinking what a solemn thing it was to move on through the lonely darkness over an unknown abyss, whose depths were secrets as profound as death: it was a great surprise to Scrooge, while thus engaged, to hear a hearty laugh. It was a much greater surprise to Scrooge to recognise it as his own nephew's and to find himself in a bright, dry, gleaming room, with the Spirit standing smiling by his side, and looking at that same nephew with approving affability!

'Ha, ha!' laughed Scrooge's nephew. 'Ha, ha, ha!'

If you should happen, by any unlikely chance, to know a man more blessed in a laugh than Scrooge's nephew, all I can say is, I should like to know him too. Introduce him to me, and I'll cultivate his acquaintance.

It is a fair, even-handed, noble adjustment of things, that while there is infection in disease and sorrow, there is nothing in the world so irresistibly contagious as laughter and good-humour. When Scrooge's nephew laughed in this way—holding his sides, rolling his head, and twisting his face into the most extravagant contortions—Scrooge's niece, by marriage, laughed as heartily as he. And their assembled friends, being not a bit behindhand, roared out lustily.

'Ha, ha! Ha, ha, ha, ha!'

'He said that Christmas was a humbug, as I live!' cried Scrooge's nephew. 'He believed it, too!'

'More shame for him, Fred!' said Scrooge's niece indignantly. Bless those women! they never do anything by halves. They are always in earnest.

She was very pretty; exceedingly pretty. With a dimpled, surprised-looking, capital face; a ripe little mouth, that seemed made to be kissed—as no doubt it was; all kinds of good little dots about her chin, that melted into one another when she laughed; and the sunniest pair of eyes you ever saw in any little creature's head. Altogether she was what you would have called provoking, you know; but satisfactory, too. Oh, perfectly satisfactory!

'He's a comical old fellow,' said Scrooge's nephew, 'that's the truth; and not so pleasant as he might be. However, his offences carry their own punishment, and I have nothing to say against him.'

'I'm sure he is very rich, Fred,' hinted Scrooge's niece. 'At least, you always tell *me* so.'

'What of that, my dear?' said Scrooge's nephew. 'His wealth is of no use to him. He don't do any good with it. He don't make himself comfortable with it. He hasn't the satisfaction of thinking—ha, ha, ha! —that he is ever going to benefit Us with it.'

'I have no patience with him,' observed Scrooge's niece. Scrooge's niece's sisters, and all the other ladies, expressed the same opinion.

'Oh, I have!' said Scrooge's nephew. 'I am sorry for him; I couldn't be angry with him if I tried. Who suffers by his ill whims? Himself always. Here he takes it into his head to dislike us, and he won't come and dine with us. What's the consequence? He don't lose much of a dinner.'

'Indeed, I think he loses a very good dinner,' interrupted Scrooge's niece. Everybody else said the same, and they must be allowed to have been competent judges, because they had just had dinner; and with the dessert upon the table, were clustered round the fire, by lamplight.

'Well! I am very glad to hear it,' said Scrooge's nephew, 'because I haven't any great faith in these young housekeepers. What do *you* say, Topper?'

Topper had clearly got his eye upon one of Scrooge's niece's sisters, for he answered that a bachelor was a wretched outcast, who had no right to express an opinion on the subject. Whereat Scrooge's niece's sister—the plump one with the lace tucker: not the one with the roses—blushed.

'Do go on, Fred,' said Scrooge's niece, clapping her hands. 'He never finishes what he begins to say! He is such a ridiculous fellow!'

Scrooge's nephew revelled in another laugh, and as it was impossible to keep the infection off, though the plump sister tried hard to do it with aromatic vinegar, his example was unanimously followed.

'I was only going to say,' said Scrooge's nephew, 'that the consequence of his taking a dislike to us, and not making merry with us, is, as I think, that he loses some pleasant moments, which could do him no harm. I am sure he loses pleasanter companions than he can find in his own thoughts, either in his mouldy old office or his dusty chambers. I mean to give him the same chance every year, whether he likes it or not, for I pity him. He may rail at Christmas till he dies, but he can't help thinking better of it—I defy him— if he finds me going there, in good temper, year after year, and saying, "Uncle Scrooge, how are you?" If it only put him in the vein to leave his poor clerk fifty pounds, *that's* something; and I think I shook him yesterday.'

It was their turn to laugh now, at the notion of his shaking Scrooge. But being thoroughly good-natured, and not much caring what they laughed at, so that they laughed at any rate, he encouraged them in their merriment, and passed the bottle, joyously.

After tea they had some music. For they were a musical family, and knew what they were about when they sung a Glee or Catch, I can assure you: especially Topper, who could growl away in the bass like a good one, and never swell the large veins in his forehead, or get red in the face over it. Scrooge's niece played well upon the harp; and played, among other tunes, a simple little air (a mere nothing: you might learn to whistle it in two minutes) which had been familiar to the child who fetched Scrooge from the boarding-school, as he had been reminded by the Ghost of Christmas Past. When this strain of music sounded, all the things that Ghost had shown him came upon his mind; he softened more and more; and thought that if he could have listened to it often, years ago, he might have cultivated the kindnesses of life for his own happiness with his own hands, without resorting to the sexton's spade that buried Jacob Marley.

But they didn't devote the whole evening to music. After a while they played at forfeits; for it is good to be children sometimes, and never better than at Christmas, when its mighty Founder was a child himself. Stop! There was first a game at blindman's-buff. Of course there was. And I no more believe Topper was really blind than I believe he had eyes in his boots. My opinion is, that it was a done thing between him and Scrooge's nephew; and that the Ghost of Christmas Present knew it. The way he went after that plump sister in the lace tucker was an outrage on the credulity of human nature. Knocking down the fire-irons, tumbling over the chairs, bumping up against the piano, smothering himself amongst the curtains, wherever she went, there went he! He always knew where the plump sister was. He wouldn't catch anybody else. If you had fallen up against him (as some of them did) on purpose, he would have made a feint of endeavouring to seize you, which would have been an affront to your understanding, and would instantly have sidled off in the direction of the plump sister. She often cried out that it wasn't fair; and it really was not. But when, at last, he caught her; when, in spite of all her silken rustlings, and her rapid flutterings past him, he got her into a corner whence there was no escape; then his conduct was the most execrable. For his pretending not to know her; his pretending that it was necessary to touch her headdress, and further to assure himself of her identity by pressing a certain ring upon her finger, and a certain chain about her neck; was vile, monstrous! No doubt she told him her opinion of it when, another blind man being in office, they were so very confidential together behind the curtains.

Scrooge's niece was not one of the blindman's-buff party, but was made comfortable with a large chair and a footstool, in a snug corner where the Ghost and Scrooge were close behind her. But she joined in the forfeits, and loved her love to admiration with all the letters of the alphabet. Likewise at the game of How, When, and Where, she was very great, and, to the secret joy of Scrooge's nephew, beat her sisters hollow; though they were sharp girls too, as Topper could have told you. There might have been twenty people there, young and old, but they all played, and so did Scrooge; for wholly forgetting, in the interest he had in what was going on, that his voice made no sound in their ears, he sometimes came out with his guess quite loud, and very often guessed right, too; for the sharpest needle, best Whitechapel, warranted not to cut in the eye, was not sharper than Scrooge, blunt as he took it in his head to be.

The Ghost was greatly pleased to find him in this mood, and looked upon him with such favour that he begged like a boy to be allowed to stay until the guests departed. But this the Spirit said could not be done.

'Here is a new game,' said Scrooge. 'One half-hour, Spirit, only one!'

It was a game called Yes and No, where Scrooge's nephew had to think of something, and the rest must find out what, he only answering to their questions yes or no, as the case was. The brisk fire of questioning to which he was exposed elicited from him that he was thinking of an animal, a live animal, rather a disagreeable animal, a savage animal, an animal that growled and grunted sometimes, and talked sometimes and lived in London, and walked about the streets, and wasn't made a show of, and wasn't led by anybody, and didn't live in a menagerie, and was never killed in a market, and was not a horse, or an ass, or a cow, or a bull, or a tiger, or a dog, or a pig, or a cat, or a bear. At every fresh question that was put to him, this nephew burst into a fresh roar of laughter; and was so inexpressibly tickled, that he was obliged to get up off the sofa and stamp. At last the plump sister, falling into a similar state, cried out:

'I have found it out! I know what it is, Fred! I know what it is!'

'What is it?' cried Fred.

'It's your uncle Scro-o-o-o-oge.'

Which it certainly was. Admiration was the universal sentiment, though some objected that the reply to 'Is it a bear?' ought to have been 'Yes'; inasmuch as an answer in the negative was sufficient to have diverted their thoughts from Mr. Scrooge, supposing they had ever had any tendency that way.

'He has given us plenty of merriment, I am sure,' said Fred, 'and it would be ungrateful not to drink his health. Here is a glass of mulled wine ready to our hand at the moment; and I say, "Uncle Scrooge!"'

'Well! Uncle Scrooge!' they cried.

'A merry Christmas and a happy New Year to the old man, whatever he is!' said Scrooge's nephew. 'He wouldn't take it from me, but may he have it, nevertheless. Uncle Scrooge!'

Uncle Scrooge had imperceptibly become so gay and light of heart, that he would have pledged the unconscious company in return, and thanked them in an inaudible speech, if the Ghost had given him time. But the whole scene passed off in the breath of the last word spoken by his nephew; and he and the Spirit were again upon their travels.

Much they saw, and far they went, and many homes they visited, but always with a happy end. The Spirit stood beside sick-beds, and they were cheerful; on foreign lands, and they were close at home; by struggling men, and they were patient in their greater hope; by poverty, and it was rich. In almshouse, hospital, and gaol, in misery's every refuge, where vain man in his little brief authority had not made fast the door, and barred the Spirit out, he left his blessing and taught Scrooge his precepts.

It was a long night, if it were only a night; but Scrooge had his doubts of this, because the Christmas holidays appeared to be condensed into the space of time they passed together. It was strange, too, that, while Scrooge remained unaltered in his outward form, the Ghost grew older, clearly older. Scrooge had observed this change, but never spoke of it until they left a children's Twelfth-Night party, when, looking at the Spirit as they stood together in an open place, he noticed that its hair was grey.

'Are spirits' lives so short?' asked Scrooge.

'My life upon this globe is very brief,' replied the Ghost. 'It ends tonight.'

'Tonight!' cried Scrooge.

'Tonight at midnight. Hark! The time is drawing near.'

The chimes were ringing the three-quarters past eleven at that moment.

'Forgive me if I am not justified in what I ask,' said Scrooge, looking intently at the Spirit's robe, 'but I see something strange, and not belonging to yourself, protruding from your skirts. Is it a foot or a claw?'

'It might be a claw, for the flesh there is upon it,' was the Spirit's sorrowful reply. 'Look here!'

From the foldings of its robe it brought two children, wretched, abject, frightful, hideous, miserable. They knelt down at its feet, and clung upon the outside of its garment.

'O Man! look here! Look, look down here!' exclaimed the Ghost.

They were a boy and girl. Yellow, meagre, ragged, scowling, wolfish, but prostrate, too, in their humility. Where graceful youth should have filled their features out, and touched them with its freshest tints, a stale and shrivelled hand, like that of age, had pinched and twisted them, and pulled them into shreds. Where angels might have sat enthroned, devils lurked, and glared out menacing. No change, no degradation, no perversion of humanity in any grade, through all the mysteries of wonderful creation, has monsters half so horrible and dread.

Scrooge started back, appalled. Having them shown to him in this way, he tried to say they were fine children, but the words choked themselves, rather than be parties to a lie of such enormous magnitude.

'Spirit! are they yours?' Scrooge could say no more.

'They are Man's,' said the Spirit, looking down upon them. 'And they cling to me, appealing from their fathers. This boy is Ignorance. This girl is Want. Beware of them both, and all of their degree, but most of all beware this boy, for on his brow I see that written which is Doom, unless the writing be erased. Deny it!' cried the Spirit, stretching out his hand towards the city. 'Slander those who tell it ye! Admit it for your factious purposes, and make it worse! And bide the end!'

'Have they no refuge or resource?' cried Scrooge.

'Are there no prisons?' said the Spirit, turning on him for the last time with his own words. 'Are there no workhouses?'

The bell struck Twelve.

Scrooge looked about him for the Ghost, and saw it not. As the last stroke ceased to vibrate, he remembered the prediction of old Jacob Marley, and, lifting up his eyes, beheld a solemn Phantom, draped and hooded, coming like a mist along the ground towards him.

PART FOUR

THE LAST OF THE SPIRITS

The Phantom slowly, gravely, silently approached. When it came near him, Scrooge bent down upon his knee; for in the very air through which this Spirit moved it seemed to scatter gloom and mystery.

It was shrouded in a deep black garment, which concealed its head, its face, its form, and left nothing of it visible, save one outstretched hand. But for this, it would have been difficult to detach its figure from the night, and separate it from the darkness by which it was surrounded.

He felt that it was tall and stately when it came beside him, and that its mysterious presence filled him with a solemn dread. He knew no more, for the Spirit neither spoke nor moved.

'I am in the presence of the Ghost of Christmas Yet to Come?' said Scrooge.

The Spirit answered not, but pointed onward with its hand.

'You are about to show me shadows of the things that have not happened, but will happen in the time before us,' Scrooge pursued. 'Is that so, Spirit?'

The upper portion of the garment was contracted for an instant in its folds, as if the Spirit had inclined its head. That was the only answer he received.

Although well used to ghostly company by this time, Scrooge feared the silent shape so much that his legs trembled beneath him, and he found that he could hardly stand when he prepared to follow it. The Spirit paused a moment, as observing his condition, and giving him time to recover.

But Scrooge was all the worse for this. It thrilled him with a vague, uncertain horror to know that, behind the dusky shroud, there were ghostly eyes intently fixed upon him, while he, though he stretched his own to the utmost, could see nothing but a spectral hand and one great heap of black.

'Ghost of the Future!' he exclaimed, 'I fear you more than any spectre I have seen. But as I know your purpose is to do me good, and as I hope to live to be another man from what I was, I am prepared to bear your company, and do it with a thankful heart. Will you not speak to me?'

It gave him no reply. The hand was pointed straight before them.

'Lead on!' said Scrooge. 'Lead on! The night is waning fast, and it is precious time to me, I know. Lead on, Spirit!'

The Phantom moved away as it had come towards him. Scrooge followed in the shadow of its dress, which bore him up, he thought, and carried him along.

They scarcely seemed to enter the City; for the City rather seemed to spring up about them, and encompass them of its own act. But there they were in the heart of it; on 'Change, amongst the merchants, who hurried up and down, and chinked the money in their pockets, and conversed in groups, and looked at their watches, and trifled thoughtfully with their great gold seals, and so forth, as Scrooge had seen them often.

The Spirit stopped beside one little knot of business men. Observing that the hand was pointed to them, Scrooge advanced to listen to their talk.

'No,' said a great fat man with a monstrous chin, 'I don't know much about it either way. I only know he's dead.'

'When did he die?' inquired another.

'Last night, I believe.'

'Why, what was the matter with him?' asked a third, taking a vast quantity of snuff out of a very large snuff-box. 'I thought he'd never die.'

'God knows,' said the first, with a yawn.

'What has he done with his money?' asked a red-faced gentleman with a pendulous excrescence on the end of his nose, that shook like the gills of a turkey-cock.

'I haven't heard,' said the man with the large chin, yawning again. 'Left it to his company, perhaps. He hasn't left it to *me*. That's all I know.'

This pleasantry was received with a general laugh.

'It's likely to be a very cheap funeral,' said the same speaker; 'for, upon my life, I don't know of anybody to go to it. Suppose we make up a party, and volunteer?'

'I don't mind going if a lunch is provided,' observed the gentleman with the excrescence on his nose. 'But I must be fed if I make one.'

Another laugh.

'Well, I am the most disinterested among you, after all,' said the first speaker, 'for I never wear black gloves, and I never eat lunch. But I'll offer to go if anybody else will. When I come to think of it, I'm not at all sure that I wasn't his most particular friend; for we used to stop and speak whenever we met. Bye, bye!'

Speakers and listeners strolled away, and mixed with other groups. Scrooge knew the men, and looked towards the Spirit for an explanation.

The phantom glided on into a street. Its finger pointed to two persons meeting. Scrooge listened again, thinking that the explanation might lie here.

He knew these men, also, perfectly. They were men of business: very wealthy, and of great importance. He had made a point always of standing well in their esteem in a business point of view, that is; strictly in a business point of view.

'How are you?' said one.

'How are you?' returned the other.

'Well!' said the first, 'old Scratch has got his own at last, hey?'

'So I am told,' returned the second. 'Cold, isn't it?'

'Seasonable for Christmas-time. You are not a skater, I suppose?'

'No, no. Something else to think of. Good-morning!'

Not another word. That was their meeting, their conversation, and their parting.

Scrooge was at first inclined to be surprised that the Spirit should attach importance to conversations apparently so trivial; but feeling assured that they must have some hidden purpose, he set himself to consider what it was likely to be. They could scarcely be supposed to have any bearing on the death of Jacob, his old partner, for that was Past, and this Ghost's province was the Future. Nor could he think of any one immediately connected with himself to whom he could apply them. But nothing doubting that, to whomsoever they applied, they had some latent moral for his own improvement, he resolved to treasure up every word he heard, and everything he saw; and especially to observe the shadow of himself when it appeared. For he had an expectation that the conduct of his future self would give him the clue he missed, and would render the solution of these riddles easy.

He looked about in that very place for his own image, but another man stood in his accustomed corner; and though the clock pointed to his usual time of day for being there, he saw no likeness of himself among the multitudes that poured in through the Porch. It gave him little surprise, however; for he had been revolving in his mind a change of life, and thought and hoped he saw his new-born resolutions carried out in this.

Quiet and dark, beside him stood the Phantom, with its outstretched hand. When he roused himself from his thoughtful quest, he fancied, from the turn of the hand, and its situation in reference to himself, that the Unseen Eyes were looking at him keenly. It made him shudder, and feel very cold.

They left the busy scene, and went into an obscure part of the town, where Scrooge had never penetrated before, although he recognised its situation and its bad repute. The ways were foul and narrow; the shops and houses wretched; the people half naked, drunken, slipshod, ugly. Alleys and archways, like so many cesspools, disgorged their offences of smell and dirt, and life upon the straggling streets; and the whole quarter reeked with crime, with filth, and misery.

Far in this den of infamous resort, there was a lowbrowed, beetling shop, below a penthouse roof, where iron, old rags, bottles, bones, and greasy offal were bought. Upon the floor within were piled up heaps of rusty keys, nails, chains, hinges, files, scales, weights, and refuse iron of all kinds. Secrets that few would like to scrutinise were bred and hidden in mountains of unseemly rags, masses of corrupted fat, and sepulchres of bones. Sitting in among the wares he dealt in, by a charcoal stove made of old bricks, was a grey-haired rascal, nearly seventy years of age, who had screened himself from the cold air without by a frouzy curtaining of miscellaneous tatters hung upon a line and smoked his pipe in all the luxury of calm retirement.

Scrooge and the Phantom came into the presence of this man, just as a woman with a heavy bundle slunk into the shop. But she had scarcely entered, when another woman, similarly laden, came in too; and she was closely followed by a man in faded black, who was no less startled by the sight of them than they had been upon the recognition of each other. After a short period of blank astonishment, in which the old man with the pipe had joined them, they all three burst into a laugh.

'Let the charwoman alone to be the first!' cried she who had entered first. 'Let the laundress alone to be the second; and let the undertaker's man alone to be the third. Look here, old Joe, here's a chance! If we haven't all three met here without meaning it!'

'You couldn't have met in a better place,' said old Joe, removing his pipe from his mouth. 'Come into the parlour. You were made free of it long ago, you know; and the other two an't strangers. Stop till I shut the door of the shop. Ah! how it skreeks! There an't such a rusty bit of metal in the place as its own hinges, I believe; and I'm sure there's no such old bones here as mine. Ha! ha! We're all suitable to our calling, we're well matched. Come into the parlour. Come into the parlour.'

The parlour was the space behind the screen of rags. The old man raked the fire together with an old stair-rod, and having trimmed his smoky lamp (for it was night) with the stem of his pipe, put it into his mouth again.

While he did this, the woman who had already spoken threw her bundle on the floor, and sat down in a flaunting manner on a stool, crossing her elbows on her knees, and looking with a bold defiance at the other two.

'What odds, then? What odds, Mrs. Dilber?' said the woman. 'Every person has a right to take care of themselves. *He* always did!'

'That's true, indeed!' said the laundress. 'No man more so.'

'Why, then, don't stand staring as if you was afraid, woman! Who's the wiser? We're not going to pick holes in each other's coats, I suppose?'

'No, indeed!' said Mrs. Dilber and the man together, 'We should hope not.'

'Very well then!' cried the woman. 'That's enough. Who's the worse for the loss of a few things like these? Not a dead man, I suppose?'

'No, indeed,' said Mrs. Dilber, laughing.

'If he wanted to keep 'em after he was dead, a wicked old screw,' pursued the woman, 'why wasn't he natural in his lifetime? If he had been, he'd have had somebody to look after him when he was struck with Death, instead of lying gasping out his last there, alone by himself.'

'It's the truest word that ever was spoke,' said Mrs. Dilber. 'It's a judgement on him.'

'I wish it was a little heavier judgement,' replied the woman: 'and it should have been, you may depend upon it, if I could have laid my hands on anything else. Open that bundle, old Joe, and let me know the value of it. Speak out plain. I'm not afraid to be the first, nor afraid for them to see it. We knew pretty well that we were helping ourselves before we met here, I believe. It's no sin. Open the bundle, Joe.'

But the gallantry of her friends would not allow of this; and the man in faded black, mounting the breach first, produced *his* plunder. It was not extensive. A seal or two, a pencil-case, a pair of sleeve-buttons, and a brooch of no great value, were all. They were severally examined and appraised by old Joe, who chalked the sums he was disposed to give for each upon the wall, and added them up into a total when he found that there was nothing more to come.

'That's your account,' said Joe, 'and I wouldn't give another sixpence, if I was to be boiled for not doing it. Who's next?'

Mrs. Dilber was next. Sheets and towels, a little wearing apparel, two old-fashioned silver teaspoons, a pair of sugar-tongs, and a few boots. Her account was stated on the wall in the same manner.

'I always give too much to ladies. It's a weakness of mine, and that's the way I ruin myself,' said old Joe. 'That's your account. If you asked me for another penny, and made it an open question, I'd repent of being so liberal, and knock off half-a-crown.'

'And now undo *my* bundle, Joe,' said the first woman.

Joe went down on his knees for the greater convenience of opening it, and, having unfastened a great many knots, dragged out a large heavy roll of some dark stuff.

'What do you call this?' said Joe. 'Bed-curtains?'

'Ah!' returned the woman, laughing and leaning forward on her crossed arms. 'Bed-curtains!'

'You don't mean to say you took 'em down, rings and all, with him lying there?' said Joe.

'Yes, I do,' replied the woman. 'Why not?'

'You were born to make your fortune,' said Joe, 'and you'll certainly do it.'

'I certainly shan't hold my hand, when I can get anything in it by reaching it out, for the sake of such a man as he was, I promise you, Joe,' returned the woman coolly. 'Don't drop that oil upon the blankets, now.'

'His blankets?' asked Joe.

'Whose else's do you think?' replied the woman. 'He isn't likely to take cold without 'em, I dare say.'

'I hope he didn't die of anything catching? Eh?' said old Joe, stopping in his work, and looking up.

'Don't you be afraid of that,' returned the woman. 'I an't so fond of his company that I'd loiter about him for such things, if he did. Ah! you may look through that shirt till your eyes ache, but you won't find a hole in it, nor a threadbare place. It's the best he had, and a fine one too. They'd have wasted it, if it hadn't been for me.'

'What do you call wasting of it?' asked old Joe.

'Putting it on him to be buried in, to be sure,' replied the woman, with a laugh. 'Somebody was fool enough to do it, but I took it off again. If calico an't good enough for such a purpose, it isn't good enough for anything. It's quite as becoming to the body. He can't look uglier than he did in that one.'

Scrooge listened to this dialogue in horror. As they sat grouped about their spoil, in the scanty light afforded by the old man's lamp, he viewed them with a detestation and disgust which could hardly have been greater, though they had been obscene demons marketing the corpse itself.

'Ha, ha!' laughed the same woman when old Joe producing a flannel bag with money in it, told out their several gains upon the ground. 'This is the end of it, you see! He frightened every one away from him when he was alive, to profit us when he was dead! Ha, ha, ha!'

'Spirit!' said Scrooge, shuddering from head to foot. 'I see, I see. The case of this unhappy man might be my own. My life tends that way now. Merciful heaven, what is this?'

He recoiled in terror, for the scene had changed, and now he almost touched a bed—a bare, uncurtained bed—on which, beneath a ragged sheet, there lay a something covered up, which, though it was dumb, announced itself in awful language.

The room was very dark, too dark to be observed with any accuracy, though Scrooge glanced round it in obedience to a secret impulse, anxious to know what kind of room it was. A pale light, rising in the outer air, fell straight upon the bed; and on it, plundered and bereft, unwatched, unwept, uncared for, was the body of this man.

Scrooge glanced towards the Phantom. Its steady hand was pointed to the head. The cover was so carelessly adjusted that the slightest raising of it, the motion of a finger upon Scrooge's part, would have disclosed the face. He thought of it, felt how easy it would be to do, and longed to do it; but he had no more power to withdraw the veil than to dismiss the spectre at his side.

Oh, cold, cold, rigid, dreadful Death, set up thine altar here, and dress it with such terrors as thou hast at thy command; for this is thy dominion! But of the loved, revered, and honoured head thou canst not turn one hair to thy dread purposes, or make one feature odious. It is not that the hand is heavy, and will fall down when released; it is not that the heart and pulse are still; but that the hand was open, generous, and true; the heart brave, warm, and tender, and the pulse a man's. Strike, Shadow, strike! And see his good deeds springing from the wound, to sow the world with life immortal!

No voice pronounced these words in Scrooge's ears, and yet he heard them when he looked upon the bed. He thought, if this man could be raised up now, what would be his foremost thoughts? Avarice, hard dealing, griping cares? They have brought him to a rich end, truly!

He lay in the dark, empty house, with not a man, a woman, or a child to say he was kind to me in this or that, and for the memory of one kind word I will be kind to him. A cat was tearing at the door, and there was a sound of gnawing rats beneath the hearthstone. What *they* wanted in the room of death, and why they were so restless and disturbed, Scrooge did not dare to think.

'Spirit!' he said, 'this is a fearful place. In leaving it, I shall not leave its lesson, trust me. Let us go!'

Still the Ghost pointed with an unmoved finger to the head.

'I understand you,' Scrooge returned, 'and I would do it if I could. But I have not the power, Spirit. I have not the power.'

Again it seemed to look upon him.

'If there is any person in the town who feels emotion caused by this man's death,' said Scrooge, quite agonised, 'show that person to me, Spirit, I beseech you!'

The Phantom spread its dark robe before him for a moment, like a wing; and, withdrawing it, revealed a room by daylight, where a mother and her children were.

She was expecting some one, and with anxious eagerness; for she walked up and down the room, started at every sound, looked out from the window, glanced at the clock, tried, but in vain, to work with her needle, and could hardly bear the voices of her children in their play.

At length the long-expected knock was heard. She hurried to the door, and met her husband; a man whose face was careworn and depressed, though he was young. There was a remarkable expression in it now, a kind of serious delight of which he felt ashamed, and which he struggled to repress.

He sat down to the dinner that had been hoarding for him by the fire, and when she asked him faintly what news (which was not until after a long silence), he appeared embarrassed how to answer.

'Is it good,' she said, 'or bad?' to help him.

'Bad,' he answered

'We are quite ruined?'

'No. There is hope yet, Caroline.'

'If *he* relents,' she said, amazed, 'there is! Nothing is past hope, if such a miracle has happened.'

'He is past relenting,' said her husband. 'He is dead.'

She was a mild and patient creature, if her face spoke truth; but she was thankful in her soul to hear it, and she said so with clasped hands. She prayed forgiveness the next moment, and was sorry; but the first was the emotion of her heart.

'What the half-drunken woman, whom I told you of last night, said to me when I tried to see him and obtain a week's delay   and what I thought was a mere excuse to avoid me—turns out to have been quite true. He was not only very ill, but dying, then.'

'To whom will our debt be transferred?'

'I don't know. But, before that time, we shall be ready with the money; and even though we were not, it would be bad fortune indeed to find so merciless a creditor in his successor. We may sleep tonight with light hearts, Caroline!'

Yes. Soften it as they would, their hearts were lighter. The children's faces, hushed and clustered round to hear what they so little understood, were brighter; and it was a happier house for this man's death! The only emotion that the Ghost could show him, caused by the event, was one of pleasure.

'Let me see some tenderness connected with a death,' said Scrooge; 'or that dark chamber, Spirit, which we left just now, will be for ever present to me.'

The Ghost conducted him through several streets familiar to his feet; and as they went along, Scrooge looked here and there to find himself, but nowhere was he to be seen. They entered poor Bob Cratchit's house; the dwelling he had visited before; and found the mother and the children seated round the fire.

Quiet. Very quiet. The noisy little Cratchits were as still as statues in one corner, and sat looking up at Peter, who had a book before him. The mother and her daughters were engaged in sewing. But surely they were very quiet!

'"And he took a child, and set him in the midst of them."'

Where had Scrooge heard those words? He had not dreamed them. The boy must have read them out as he and the Spirit crossed the threshold. Why did he not go on?

The mother laid her work upon the table, and put her hand up to her face.

'The colour hurts my eyes,' she said.

The colour? Ah, poor Tiny Tim!

'They're better now again,' said Cratchit's wife. 'It makes them weak by candle-light; and I wouldn't show weak eyes to your father when he comes home for the world. It must be near his time.'

'Past it rather,' Peter answered, shutting up his book. 'But I think he has walked a little slower than he used, these few last evenings, mother.'

They were very quiet again. At last she said, and in a steady, cheerful voice, that only faltered once:

'I have known him walk with—I have known him walk with Tiny Tim upon his shoulder very fast indeed.'

'And so have I,' cried Peter. 'Often.'

'And so have I,' exclaimed another. So had all.

'But he was very light to carry,' she resumed, intent upon her work, 'and his father loved him so, that it was no trouble, no trouble. And there is your father at the door!'

She hurried out to meet him; and little Bob in his comforter—he had need of it, poor fellow—came in. His tea was ready for him on the hob, and they all tried who should help him to it most. Then the two young Cratchits got upon his knees, and laid, each child, a little cheek against his face, as if they said, 'Don't mind it, father. Don't be grieved!'

Bob was very cheerful with them, and spoke pleasantly to all the family. He looked at the work upon the table, and praised the industry and speed of Mrs. Cratchit and the girls. They would be done long before Sunday, he said.

'Sunday! You went today, then, Robert?' said his wife.

'Yes, my dear,' returned Bob. 'I wish you could have gone. It would have done you good to see how green a place it is. But you'll see it often. I promised him that I would walk there on a Sunday. My little, little child!' cried Bob. 'My little child!'

He broke down all at once. He couldn't help it. If he could have helped it, he and his child would have been farther apart, perhaps, than they were.

He left the room, and went upstairs into the room above, which was lighted cheerfully, and hung with Christmas. There was a chair set close beside the child, and there were signs of some one having been there lately. Poor Bob sat down in it, and when he had thought a little and composed himself, he kissed the little face. He was reconciled to what had happened, and went down again quite happy.

They drew about the fire, and talked, the girls and mother working still. Bob told them of the extraordinary kindness of Mr. Scrooge's nephew, whom he had scarcely seen but once, and who, meeting him in the street that day, and seeing that he looked a little—'just a little down, you know,' said Bob, inquired what had happened to distress him. 'On which,' said Bob, 'for he is the pleasantest-spoken gentleman you ever heard, I told him. "I am heartily sorry for it, Mr. Cratchit," he said, "and heartily sorry for your good wife." By-the-bye, how he ever knew *that* I don't know.'

'Knew what, my dear?'

'Why, that you were a good wife,' replied Bob.

'Everybody knows that,' said Peter.

'Very well observed, my boy!' cried Bob. 'I hope they do. "Heartily sorry," he said, "for your good wife. If I can be of service to you in any way," he said, giving me his card, "that's where I live. Pray come to me." Now, it wasn't,' cried Bob, 'for the sake of anything he might be able to do for us, so much as for his kind way, that this was quite delightful. It really seemed as if he had known our Tiny Tim, and felt with us.'

'I'm sure he's a good soul!' said Mrs. Cratchit.

'You would be sure of it, my dear,' returned Bob, 'if you saw and spoke to him. I shouldn't be at all surprised—mark what I say!—if he got Peter a better situation.'

'Only hear that, Peter,' said Mrs. Cratchit.

'And then,' cried one of the girls, 'Peter will be keeping company with some one, and setting up for himself.'

'Get along with you!' retorted Peter, grinning.

'It's just as likely as not,' said Bob, 'one of these days; though there's plenty of time for that, my dear. But, however and whenever we part from one another, I am sure we shall none of us forget poor Tiny Tim—shall we—or this first parting that there was among us?'

'Never, father!' cried they all.

'And I know,' said Bob, 'I know, my dears, that when we recollect how patient and how mild he was; although he was a little, little child; we shall not quarrel easily among ourselves, and forget poor Tiny Tim in doing it.'

'No, never, father!' they all cried again.

'I am very happy,' said little Bob, 'I am very happy!'

Mrs. Cratchit kissed him, his daughters kissed him, the two young Cratchits kissed him, and Peter and himself shook hands. Spirit of Tiny Tim, thy childish essence was from God!

'Spectre,' said Scrooge, 'something informs me that our parting moment is at hand. I know it but I know not how. Tell me what man that was whom we saw lying dead?'

The Ghost of Christmas Yet to Come conveyed him, as before—though at a different time, he thought: indeed there seemed no order in these latter visions, save that they were in the Future—into the resorts of business men, but showed him not himself. Indeed, the Spirit did not stay for anything, but went straight on, as to the end just now desired, until besought by Scrooge to tarry for a moment.

'This court,' said Scrooge, 'through which we hurry now, is where my place of occupation is, and has been for a length of time. I see the house. Let me behold what I shall be in days to come.'

The Spirit stopped; the hand was pointed elsewhere.

'The house is yonder,' Scrooge exclaimed. 'Why do you point away?'

The inexorable finger underwent no change.

Scrooge hastened to the window of his office, and looked in. It was an office still, but not his. The furniture was not the same, and the figure in the chair was not himself. The Phantom pointed as before.

He joined it once again, and, wondering why and whither he had gone, accompanied it until they reached an iron gate. He paused to look round before entering.

A churchyard. Here, then, the wretched man, whose name he had now to learn, lay underneath the ground. It was a worthy place. Walled in by houses; overrun by grass and weeds, the growth of vegetation's death, not life; choked up with too much burying; fat with repleted appetite. A worthy place!

The Spirit stood among the graves, and pointed down to One. He advanced towards it trembling. The Phantom was exactly as it had been, but he dreaded that he saw new meaning in its solemn shape.

'Before I draw nearer to that stone to which you point,' said Scrooge, 'answer me one question. Are these the shadows of the things that Will be, or are they shadows of the things that May be only?'

Still the Ghost pointed downward to the grave by which it stood.

'Men's courses will foreshadow certain ends, to which, if persevered in, they must lead,' said Scrooge. 'But if the courses be departed from, the ends will change. Say it is thus with what you show me!'

The Spirit was immovable as ever.

Scrooge crept towards it, trembling as he went; and, following the finger, read upon the stone of the neglected grave his own name, EBENEZER SCROOGE.

'Am *I* that man who lay upon the bed?' he cried upon his knees.

The finger pointed from the grave to him, and back again.

'No, Spirit! Oh no, no!'

The finger still was there.

'Spirit!' he cried, tight clutching at its robe, 'hear me! I am not the man I was. I will not be the man I must have been but for this intercourse. Why show me this, if I am past all hope?'

For the first time the hand appeared to shake.

'Good Spirit,' he pursued, as down upon the ground he fell before it, 'your nature intercedes for me, and pities me. Assure me that I yet may change these shadows you have shown me by an altered life?'

The kind hand trembled.

'I will honour Christmas in my heart, and try to keep it all the year. I will live in the Past, the Present, and the Future. The Spirits of all Three shall strive within me. I will not shut out the lessons that they teach. Oh, tell me I may sponge away the writing on this stone!'

In his agony he caught the spectral hand. It sought to free itself, but he was strong in his entreaty, and detained it. The Spirit stronger yet, repulsed him.

Holding up his hands in a last prayer to have his fate reversed, he saw an alteration in the Phantom's hood and dress. It shrunk, collapsed, and dwindled down into a bed-post.

PART FIVE

THE END OF IT

Yes! and the bedpost was his own. The bed was his own, the room was his own. Best and happiest of all, the Time before him was his own, to make amends in!

'I will live in the Past, the Present, and the Future!' Scrooge repeated as he scrambled out of bed. 'The Spirits of all Three shall strive within me. O Jacob Marley! Heaven and the Christmas Time be praised for this! I say it on my knees, old Jacob; on my knees!'

He was so fluttered and so glowing with his good intentions, that his broken voice would scarcely answer to his call. He had been sobbing violently in his conflict with the Spirit, and his face was wet with tears.

'They are not torn down,' cried Scrooge, folding one of his bed-curtains in his arms, 'They are not torn down, rings and all. They are here—I am here—the shadows of the things that would have been may be dispelled. They will be. I know they will!'

His hands were busy with his garments all this time: turning them inside out, putting them on upside down, tearing them, mislaying them, making them parties to every kind of extravagance.

'I don't know what to do!' cried Scrooge, laughing and crying in the same breath, and making a perfect Laocoon of himself with his stockings. 'I am as light as a feather, I am as happy as an angel, I am as merry as a schoolboy, I am as giddy as a drunken man. A merry Christmas to everybody! A happy New Year to all the world! Hallo here! Whoop! Hallo!'

He had frisked into the sitting-room, and was now standing there, perfectly winded.

'There's the saucepan that the gruel was in!' cried Scrooge, starting off again, and going round the fireplace. 'There's the door by which the Ghost of Jacob Marley entered! There's the corner where the Ghost of Christmas Present sat! There's the window where I saw the wandering Spirits! It's all right, it's all true, it all happened. Ha, ha, ha!'

Really, for a man who had been out of practise for so many years, it was a splendid laugh, a most illustrious laugh. The father of a long, long line of brilliant laughs!

'I don't know what day of the month it is,' said Scrooge. 'I don't know how long I have been among the Spirits. I don't know anything. I'm quite a baby. Never mind. I don't care. I'd rather be a baby. Hallo! Whoop! Hallo here!'

He was checked in his transports by the churches ringing out the lustiest peals he had ever heard. Clash, clash, hammer; ding, dong, bell! Bell, dong, ding; hammer, clash, clash! Oh, glorious, glorious!

Running to the window, he opened it, and put out his head. No fog, no mist; clear, bright, jovial, stirring, cold; cold, piping for the blood to dance to; golden sunlight; heavenly sky; sweet fresh air; merry bells. Oh, glorious! Glorious!

'What's today?' cried Scrooge, calling downward to a boy in Sunday clothes, who perhaps had loitered in to look about him.

'Eh?' returned the boy with all his might of wonder.

'What's today, my fine fellow?' said Scrooge.

'Today!' replied the boy. 'Why, CHRISTMAS DAY.'

'It's Christmas Day!' said Scrooge to himself. 'I haven't missed it. The Spirits have done it all in one night. They can do anything they like. Of course they can. Of course they can. Hallo, my fine fellow!'

'Hallo!' returned the boy.

'Do you know the poulterer's in the next street but one, at the corner?' Scrooge inquired.

'I should hope I did,' replied the lad.

'An intelligent boy!' said Scrooge. 'A remarkable boy! Do you know whether they've sold the prize turkey that was hanging up there?—Not the little prize turkey: the big one?'

'What! the one as big as me?' returned the boy.

'What a delightful boy!' said Scrooge. 'It's a pleasure to talk to him. Yes, my buck!'

'It's hanging there now,' replied the boy.

'Is it?' said Scrooge. 'Go and buy it.'

'Walk-in!' exclaimed the boy.

'No, no,' said Scrooge. 'I am in earnest. Go and buy it, and tell 'em to bring it here, that I may give them the directions where to take it. Come back with the man, and I'll give you a shilling. Come back with him in less than five minutes, and I'll give you half-a-crown!'

The boy was off like a shot. He must have had a steady hand at a trigger who could have got a shot off half as fast.

'I'll send it to Bob Cratchit's,' whispered Scrooge, rubbing his hands, and splitting with a laugh. 'He shan't know who sends it. It's twice the size of Tiny Tim. Joe Miller never made such a joke as sending it to Bob's will be!'

The hand in which he wrote the address was not a steady one; but write it he did, somehow, and went downstairs to open the street-door, ready for the coming of the poulterer's man. As he stood there, waiting his arrival, the knocker caught his eye.

'I shall love it as long as I live!' cried Scrooge, patting it with his hand. 'I scarcely ever looked at it before. What an honest expression it has in its face! It's a wonderful knocker!—Here's the turkey. Hallo! Whoop! How are you! Merry Christmas!'

It *was* a turkey! He never could have stood upon his legs, that bird. He would have snapped 'em short off in a minute, like sticks of sealing-wax.

'Why, it's impossible to carry that to Camden Town,' said Scrooge. 'You must have a cab.'

The chuckle with which he said this, and the chuckle with which he paid for the turkey, and the chuckle with which he paid for the cab, and the chuckle with which he recompensed the boy, were only to be exceeded by the chuckle with which he sat down breathless in his chair again, and chuckled till he cried.

Shaving was not an easy task, for his hand continued to shake very much; and shaving requires attention, even when you don't dance while you are at it. But if he had cut the end of his nose off, he would have put a piece of sticking-plaster over it, and been quite satisfied.

He dressed himself 'all in his best,' and at last got out into the streets. The people were by this time pouring forth, as he had seen them with the Ghost of Christmas Present; and, walking with his hands behind him, Scrooge regarded every one with a delighted smile. He looked so irresistibly pleasant, in a word, that three or four good-humoured fellows said, 'Good-morning, sir! A merry Christmas to you! And Scrooge said often afterwards that, of all the blithe sounds he had ever heard, those were the blithest in his ears.

He had not gone far when, coming on towards him, he beheld the portly gentleman who had walked into his counting-house the day before, and said, 'Scrooge and Marley's, I believe?' It sent a pang across his heart to think how this old gentleman would look upon him when they met; but he knew what path lay straight before him, and he took it.

'My dear sir,' said Scrooge, quickening his pace, and taking the old gentleman by both his hands, 'how do you do? I hope you succeeded yesterday. It was very kind of you. A merry Christmas to you, sir!'

'Mr. Scrooge?'

'Yes,' said Scrooge. 'That is my name, and I fear it may not be pleasant to you. Allow me to ask your pardon. And will you have the goodness———' Here Scrooge whispered in his ear.

'Lord bless me!' cried the gentleman, as if his breath were taken away. 'My dear Mr. Scrooge, are you serious?'

'If you please,' said Scrooge. 'Not a farthing less. A great many back-payments are included in it, I assure you. Will you do me that favour?'

'My dear sir,' said the other, shaking hands with him, 'I don't know what to say to such munifi———'

'Don't say anything, please,' retorted Scrooge. 'Come and see me. Will you come and see me?'

'I will!' cried the old gentleman. And it was clear he meant to do it.

'Thankee,' said Scrooge. 'I am much obliged to you. I thank you fifty times. Bless you!'

He went to church, and walked about the streets, and watched the people hurrying to and fro, and patted the children on the head, and questioned beggars, and looked down into the kitchens of houses, and up to the windows; and found that everything could yield him pleasure. He had never dreamed that any walk—that anything—could give him so much happiness. In the afternoon he turned his steps towards his nephew's house.

He passed the door a dozen times before he had the courage to go up and knock. But he made a dash and did it.

'Is your master at home, my dear?' said Scrooge to the girl. 'Nice girl! Very.'

'Yes, sir.'

'Where is he, my love?' said Scrooge.

'He's in the dining-room, sir, along with mistress. I'll show you upstairs, if you please.'

'Thankee. He knows me,' said Scrooge, with his hand already on the dining-room lock. 'I'll go in here, my dear.'

He turned it gently, and sidled his face in round the door. They were looking at the table (which was spread out in great array); for these young housekeepers are always nervous on such points, and like to see that everything is right.

'Fred!' said Scrooge.

Dear heart alive, how his niece by marriage started! Scrooge had forgotten, for the moment, about her sitting in the corner with the footstool, or he wouldn't have done it on any account.

'Why, bless my soul!' cried Fred, 'who's that?'

'It's I. Your uncle Scrooge. I have come to dinner. Will you let me in, Fred?'

Let him in! It is a mercy he didn't shake his arm off. He was at home in five minutes. Nothing could be heartier. His niece looked just the same. So did Topper when *he* came. So did the plump sister when *she* came. So did every one when *they* came. Wonderful party, wonderful games, wonderful unanimity, won-der-ful happiness!

But he was early at the office next morning. Oh, he was early there! If he could only be there first, and catch Bob Cratchit coming late! That was the thing he had set his heart upon.

And he did it; yes, he did! The clock struck nine. No Bob. A quarter past. No Bob. He was full eighteen minutes and a half behind his time. Scrooge sat with his door wide open, that he might see him come into the tank.

His hat was off before he opened the door; his comforter too. He was on his stool in a jiffy, driving away with his pen, as if he were trying to overtake nine o'clock.

'Hallo!' growled Scrooge in his accustomed voice as near as he could feign it. 'What do you mean by coming here at this time of day?'

'I am very sorry, sir,' said Bob, 'I *am* behind my time.'

'You are!' repeated Scrooge. 'Yes, I think you are. Step this way, sir, if you please.'

'It's only once a year, sir,' pleaded Bob, appearing from the tank. 'It shall not be repeated. I was making rather merry yesterday, sir.'

'Now, I'll tell you what, my friend,' said Scrooge. 'I am not going to stand this sort of thing any longer. And therefore,' he continued, leaping from his stool, and giving Bob such a dig in the waistcoat that he staggered back into the tank again—'and therefore I am about to raise your salary!'

Bob trembled, and got a little nearer to the ruler. He had a momentary idea of knocking Scrooge down with it, holding him, and calling to the people in the court for help and a strait-waistcoat.

'A merry Christmas, Bob!' said Scrooge, with an earnestness that could not be mistaken, as he clapped him on the back. 'A merrier Christmas, Bob, my good fellow, than I have given you for many a year! I'll raise your salary, and endeavour to assist your struggling family, and we will discuss your affairs this very afternoon, over a Christmas bowl of smoking bishop, Bob! Make up the fires and buy another coal-scuttle before you dot another i, Bob Cratchit!'

Scrooge was better than his word. He did it all, and infinitely more; and to Tiny Tim, who did NOT die, he was a second father. He became as good a friend, as good a master, and as good a man as the good old City knew, or any other good old city, town, or borough in the good old world. Some people laughed to see the alteration in him, but he let them laugh, and little heeded them; for he was wise enough to know that nothing ever happened on this globe, for good, at which some people did not have their fill of laughter in the outset; and knowing that such as these would be blind anyway, he thought it quite as well that they should wrinkle up their eyes in grins as have the malady in less attractive forms. His own heart laughed, and that was quite enough for him.

He had no further intercourse with Spirits, but lived upon the Total-Abstinence Principle ever afterwards; and it was always said of him that he knew how to keep Christmas well, if any man alive possessed the knowledge. May that be truly said of us, and all of us! And so, as Tiny Tim observed, God bless Us, Every One!

About the Author

CHARLES DICKENS (1812–1870) started out as a political journalist for *The Mirror of Parliament*, writing articles on parliamentary dates and election campaigns. After publishing *The Pickwick Papers* in 1836, the English writer became famous as a storyteller and went on to publish some of the most enduring novels and stories in literature.

A Bit of History

At the time of writing *A Christmas Carol*, the British people were revisiting and re-evaluating their past Christmas traditions. The Christmas tree was popularized by Queen Victoria and Prince Albert, and a revitalized interest in Christmas carols started to form. Dickens himself had written several other Christmas stories before *A Christmas Carol*, but what most directly inspired its thematic elements was his visit to the Field Lane Ragged School, a place dedicated to the free education of London's starving and illiterate street children. The treatment of the poor became a central element of *A Christmas Carol* as Scrooge attempts to redeem himself into a more sympathetic character.

Published on Christmas Eve in 1843, thirteen editions of *A Christmas Carol* were released before the end of 1844. With a variety of adaptions, it remains one of the most recognizable and celebrated Christmas stories.

THE GIFT OF THE MAGI

By O. Henry

One dollar and eighty-seven cents. That was all. And sixty cents of it was in pennies. Pennies saved one and two at a time by bulldozing the grocer and the vegetable man and the butcher until one's cheeks burned with the silent imputation of parsimony that such close dealing implied. Three times Della counted it. One dollar and eighty-seven cents. And the next day would be Christmas.

There was clearly nothing to do but flop down on the shabby little couch and howl. So Della did it. Which instigates the moral reflection that life is made up of sobs, sniffles, and smiles, with sniffles predominating.

While the mistress of the home is gradually subsiding from the first stage to the second, take a look at the home. A furnished flat at $8 per week. It did not exactly beggar description, but it certainly had that word on the lookout for the mendicancy squad.

In the vestibule below was a letterbox into which no letter would go, and an electric button from which no mortal finger could coax a ring. Also appertaining thereunto was a card bearing the name "Mr. James Dillingham Young."

The "Dillingham" had been flung to the breeze during a former period of prosperity when its possessor was being paid $30 per week. Now, when the income was shrunk to $20, though, they were thinking seriously of contracting to a modest and unassuming D. But whenever Mr. James Dillingham Young came home and reached his flat above he was called "Jim" and greatly hugged by Mrs. James Dillingham Young, already introduced to you as Della. Which is all very good.

Della finished her cry and attended to her cheeks with the powder rag. She stood by the window and looked out dully at a gray cat walking a gray fence in a gray backyard. Tomorrow would be Christmas Day, and she had only $1.87 with which to buy Jim a present. She had been saving every penny she could for months, with this result. Twenty dollars a week doesn't go far. Expenses had been greater than she had calculated. They always are. Only $1.87 to buy a present for Jim. Her Jim. Many a happy hour she had spent planning for something nice for him. Something fine and rare and sterling—something just a little bit near to being worthy of the honor of being owned by Jim.

There was a pier-glass between the windows of the room. Perhaps you have seen a pier-glass in an $8 flat. A very thin and very agile person may, by observing his reflection in a rapid sequence of longitudinal strips, obtain a fairly accurate conception of his looks. Della, being slender, had mastered the art.

Suddenly she whirled from the window and stood before the glass. Her eyes were shining brilliantly, but her face had lost its color within twenty seconds. Rapidly she pulled down her hair and let it fall to its full length.

Now, there were two possessions of the James Dillingham Youngs in which they both took a mighty pride. One was Jim's gold watch that had been his father's and his grandfather's. The other was Della's hair. Had the Queen of Sheba lived in the flat across the airshaft, Della would have let her hair hang out the window someday to dry just to depreciate Her Majesty's jewels and gifts. Had King Solomon been the janitor, with all his treasures piled up in the basement, Jim would have pulled out his watch every time he passed, just to see him pluck at his beard from envy.

So now Della's beautiful hair fell about her, rippling and shining like a cascade of brown waters. It reached below her knee and made itself almost a garment for her. And then she did it up again nervously and quickly. Once she faltered for a minute and stood still while a tear or two splashed on the worn red carpet.

On went her old brown jacket; on went her old brown hat. With a whirl of skirts and with the brilliant sparkle still in her eyes, she fluttered out the door and down the stairs to the street.

Where she stopped the sign read: "Mme. Sofronie. Hair Goods of All Kinds." One flight up Della ran, and collected herself, panting. Madame, large, too white, chilly, hardly looked the "Sofronie."

"Will you buy my hair?" asked Della.

"I buy hair," said Madame. "Take yer hat off and let's have a sight at the looks of it."

Down rippled the brown cascade.

"Twenty dollars," said Madame, lifting the mass with a practiced hand.

"Give it to me quick," said Della.

Oh, and the next two hours tripped by on rosy wings. Forget the hashed metaphor. She was ransacking the stores for Jim's present.

She found it at last. It surely had been made for Jim and no one else. There was no other like it in any of the stores, and she had turned all of them inside out. It was a platinum fob chain simple and chaste in design, properly proclaiming its value by substance alone and not by meretricious ornamentation—as all good things should do. It was even worthy of The Watch. As soon as she saw it she knew that it must be Jim's. It was like him. Quietness and value—the description applied to both. Twenty-one dollars they took from her for it, and she hurried home with the 87 cents. With that chain on his watch Jim might be properly anxious about the time in any company. Grand as the watch was, he sometimes looked at it on the sly on account of the old leather strap that he used in place of a chain.

When Della reached home her intoxication gave way a little to prudence and reason. She got out her curling irons and lighted the gas and went to work repairing the ravages made by generosity added to love. Which is always a tremendous task, dear friends—a mammoth task.

Within forty minutes her head was covered with tiny, close-lying curls that made her look wonderfully like a truant schoolboy. She looked at her reflection in the mirror long, carefully, and critically.

"If Jim doesn't kill me," she said to herself, "before he takes a second look at me, he'll say I look like a Coney Island chorus girl. But what could I do—oh! what could I do with a dollar and eighty-seven cents?"

At 7 o'clock the coffee was made and the frying pan was on the back of the stove hot and ready to cook the chops.

Jim was never late. Della doubled the fob chain in her hand and sat on the corner of the table near the door that he always entered. Then she heard his step on the stair away down on the first flight, and she turned white for just a moment. She had a habit for saying little silent prayer about the simplest everyday things, and now she whispered: "Please God, make him think I am still pretty."

The door opened and Jim stepped in and closed it. He looked thin and very serious. Poor fellow, he was only twenty-two—and to be burdened with a family! He needed a new overcoat and he was without gloves.

Jim stopped inside the door, as immovable as a setter at the scent of quail. His eyes were fixed upon Della, and there was an expression in them that she could not read, and it terrified her. It was not anger, nor surprise, nor disapproval, nor horror, nor any of the sentiments that she had been prepared for. He simply stared at her fixedly with that peculiar expression on his face.

Della wriggled off the table and went for him.

"Jim, darling," she cried, "don't look at me that way. I had my hair cut off and sold because I couldn't have lived through Christmas without giving you a present. It'll grow out again—you won't mind, will you? I just had to do it. My hair grows awfully fast. Say 'Merry Christmas!' Jim, and let's be happy. You don't know what a nice—what a beautiful, nice gift I've got for you."

"You've cut off your hair?" asked Jim, laboriously, as if he had not arrived at that patent fact yet even after the hardest mental labor.

"Cut it off and sold it," said Della. "Don't you like me just as well, anyhow? I'm me without my hair, ain't I?"

Jim looked about the room curiously.

"You say your hair is gone?" he said, with an air almost of idiocy.

"You needn't look for it," said Della. "It's sold, I tell you—sold and gone, too. It's Christmas Eve, boy. Be good to me, for it went for you. Maybe the hairs of my head were numbered," she went on with sudden serious sweetness, "but nobody could ever count my love for you. Shall I put the chops on, Jim?"

Out of his trance Jim seemed quickly to wake. He enfolded his Della. For ten seconds let us regard with discreet scrutiny some inconsequential object in the other direction. Eight dollars a week or a million a year—what is the difference? A mathematician or a wit would give you the wrong answer. The magi brought valuable gifts, but that was not among them. This dark assertion will be illuminated later on.

Jim drew a package from his overcoat pocket and threw it upon the table.

"Don't make any mistake, Dell," he said, "about me. I don't think there's anything in the way of a haircut or a shave or a shampoo that could make me like my girl any less. But if you'll unwrap that package you may see why you had me going a while at first."

White fingers and nimble tore at the string and paper. And then an ecstatic scream of joy; and then, alas! a quick feminine change to hysterical tears and wails, necessitating the immediate employment of all the comforting powers of the lord of the flat.

For there lay The Combs—the set of combs, side and back, that Della had worshipped long in a Broadway window. Beautiful combs, pure tortoise shell, with jeweled rims—just the shade to wear in the beautiful vanished hair. They were expensive combs, she knew, and her heart had simply craved and yearned over them without the least hope of possession. And now, they were hers, but the tresses that should have adorned the coveted adornments were gone.

But she hugged them to her bosom, and at length she was able to look up with dim eyes and a smile and say: "My hair grows so fast, Jim!"

And them Della leaped up like a little singed cat and cried, "Oh, oh!"

Jim had not yet seen his beautiful present. She held it out to him eagerly upon her open palm. The dull precious metal seemed to flash with a reflection of her bright and ardent spirit.

"Isn't it a dandy, Jim? I hunted all over town to find it. You'll have to look at the time a hundred times a day now. Give me your watch. I want to see how it looks on it."

Instead of obeying, Jim tumbled down on the couch and put his hands under the back of his head and smiled.

"Dell," said he, "let's put our Christmas presents away and keep 'em a while. They're too nice to use just at present. I sold the watch to get the money to buy your combs. And now suppose you put the chops on."

The magi, as you know, were wise men—wonderfully wise men—who brought gifts to the Babe in the manger. They invented the art of giving Christmas presents. Being wise, their gifts were no doubt wise ones, possibly bearing the privilege of exchange in case of duplication. And here I have lamely related to you the uneventful chronicle of two foolish children in a flat who most unwisely sacrificed for each other the greatest treasures of their house. But in a last word to the wise of these days let it be said that of all who give gifts these two were the wisest. O all who give and receive gifts, such as they are wisest. Everywhere they are wisest. They are the magi.

About the Author

WILLIAM SYDNEY PORTER (1862–1910), known by his pen name O. Henry, worked a variety of jobs ranging from pharmacist to draftsman to bookkeeper before he started writing as a regular contributor to *The Rolling Stone*. Throughout his lifetime Porter wrote hundreds of short stories, and he is the namesake of the O. Henry Prize, awarded annually for exceptional short stories.

A BIT OF HISTORY

"The Gift of the Magi" was written by O. Henry in about two hours, after *New York World* sent an office assistant to his door to receive a contribution for their Christmas edition. Despite the speed of its writing, the story still encapsulates O. Henry's most prolific literary elements and stellar prose and solidified itself as one of the most famous Christmas stories. Notable in "The Gift of the Magi" is the usage of irony, as both sides of the young couple sacrifice their most prized possessions for one another's gifts, thus rendering them useless. But O. Henry suggests that their "foolish" sacrifice is indicative of their wisdom and love for each other, a lesson that still resonates.

The First Noel

Words: Traditional English carol, possibly dating from as early as the 13th Century.
Music: 'The First Noel' Traditional English carol, possibly dating from as early as the 13th Century.
Setting: "The Methodist Sunday School Hymnal", 1911.
copyright: public domain. This score is a part of the Open Hymnal Project, 2006 Revision.

Hark! The Herald Angels Sing

CHRISTMAS

Words: Charles Wesley, 1739, alt.
Music: 'Mendelssohn' from 'Festgesang' Felix Mendelssohn, 1840. Setting: William H. Cummings, 1857.
copyright: public domain. This score is a part of the Open Hymnal Project, 2005 Revision.

1. Hark! The her - ald an - gels sing, "Glo - ry to the new - born King;
2. Christ, by high - est Heav'n a - dored; Christ the ev - er - last - ing Lord;
3. Hail the heav'n - ly Prince of Peace! Hail the Sun of Right - eous - ness!
4. Come, De - sire of na - tions, come, Fix in us Thy hum - ble home;
5. Ad - am's like - ness, Lord, ef - face, Stamp Thine im - age in its place:

Peace on earth, and mer - cy mild, God and sin - ners re - con - ciled!"
Late in time, be - hold Him come, Off - spring of a vir - gin's womb.
Light and life to all He brings, Ris'n with heal - ing in His wings.
Rise, the wo - man's con - qu'ring Seed, Bruise in us the ser - pent's head.
Se - cond Ad - am from a - bove, Re - in - state us in Thy love.

Joy - ful, all ye na - tions rise, Join the tri - umph of the skies;
Veiled in flesh the God - head see; Hail th'in - car - nate De - i - ty,
Mild He lays His glo - ry by, Born that man no more may die.
Now dis - play Thy sav - ing po - wer, Ruin - ed na - ture now re - store;
Let us Thee, though lost, re - gain, Thee, the Life, the in - ner man:

With th'an - gel - ic host pro - claim, "Christ is born in Beth - le - hem!"
Pleased with us in flesh to dwell, Je - sus our Em - man - u - el.
Born to raise the sons of earth, Born to give them se - cond birth.
Now in my - stic un - ion join Thine to ours, and ours to Thine.
O, to all Thy - self im - part, Formed in each be - liev - ing heart.

Hark! the her - ald an - gels sing, "Glo - ry to the new - born King!"

Lk 2:13-14, 1Cor 15:21-22   7 7 7 7 7 7 7 7 7 7

CHRISTMAS AT MELROSE
By Leslie Pinckney Hill

COME home with me a little space
And browse about our ancient place,
Lay by your wonted troubles here
And have a turn of Christmas cheer.
These sober walls of weathered stone
Can tell a romance of their own,
And these wide rooms of devious line
Are kindly meant in their design.
Sometimes the north wind searches through,
But be shall not be rude to you.
We'll light a log of generous girth
For winter comfort, and the mirth
Of healthy children you shall see
About a sparkling Christmas tree.
Eleanor, leader of the fold,
Hermione with heart of gold,
Elaine with comprehending eyes,
And two more yet of coddling size,
Natalie pondering all that's said,
And Mary with the cherub head—
All these shall give you sweet content
And care-destroying merriment,
While one with true Madonna grace
Moves round the glowing fireplace
Where father loves to muse aside
And grandma sits in silent pride.
And you may chafe the wasting oak,
Or freely pass the kindly joke
To mix with nuts and home-made cake
And apples set on coals to bake.
Or some fine carol we will sing
In honor of the Manger King
Or hear great Milton's organ verse
Or Plato's dialogue rehearse
What Socrates with his last breath
Sublimely said of life and death.
These dear delights we fain would share
With friend and kinsman everywhere,
And from our door see them depart
Each with a little lighter heart.

ABOUT THE AUTHOR

LESLIE PINCKNEY HILL (1880–1960) was a prolific educator, teaching at Tuskegee Institute and Manassas Industrial Institute before settling as principal of the Institute for Colored Youth. As part of the Harlem Renaissance, Hill published many poems and essays throughout his lifetime, including a play about Toussaint Louverture, the leader of the Haitian Revolution.

A Bit of History

"The world does not know that a people is great until that people produces great literature and art," says James Weldon Johnson in his preface to *The Book of American Negro Poetry*. The 1922 anthology is where "Christmas at Melrose" first appeared, selected undoubtedly for its wonderful rhythm, dynamic warm and cold imagery, and philosophical references. In one such reference, Hill recalls Socrates' final decision to die by his truth than live and have his teachings censored—a theme of exclusion that relates to African American writers of the time and the goal of the anthology itself, having largely been excluded from the literary canon. The narrator similarly ponders this idea as their Christmas dinner draws to a close and the guests walk out into the cold.

'TWAS THE NIGHT BEFORE CHRISTMAS

By Clement Clarke Moore

Twas the night before Christmas, when all through the house
Not a creature was stirring, not even a mouse.

The stockings were hung by the chimney with care,
In hopes that St. Nicholas soon would be there;

The children were nestled all snug in their beds,
while visions of sugar plums danced in their heads,

And Mama in her kerchief, and I in my cap,
Had just settled our brains for a long winter's nap-

When out on the lawn there arose such a clatter,
I sprang from my bed to see what was the matter.

Away to the window I flew like a flash,
Tore open the shutters and threw up the sash.

The moon on the breast of the new fallen snow
Gave a luster of midday to objects below,

When what to my wondering eyes did appear,
But a miniature sleigh and eight tiny reindeer,

With a little old driver so lively and quick,
I knew in a moment he must be St. Nick.

More rapid than eagles his coursers they came,
And he whistled, and shouted, and called them by name:

"Now, Dasher! Now, Dancer! Now, Prancer and Vixen!
On, Comet! On, Cupid! On, Donder and Blixen!

To the top of the porch! To the top of the wall!
Now dash away! Dash away! Dash away, all!"

As leaves that before the wild hurricane fly,
When they meet with an obstacle, mount to the sky,

So up to the housetop the coursers they flew,
With the sleigh full of toys, and St. Nicholas too—

And then, in a twinkling, I heard on the roof
The prancing and pawing of each little hoof.

As I drew in my head, and was turning around,
Down the chimney St. Nicholas came with a bound.

He was dressed all in fur, from his head to his foot,
And his clothes were all tarnished with ashes and soot;

A bundle of toys he had flung on his back,
And he looked like a peddler just opening his pack.

His eyes—how they twinkled! His dimples, how merry!
His cheeks were like roses, his nose like a cherry!

His droll little mouth was drawn up like a bow,
And the beard on his chin was as white as the snow;

The stump of a pipe he held tight in his teeth,
And the smoke, it encircled his head like a wreath;

He had a broad face and a little round belly
That shook when he laughed, like a bowl full of jelly.

He was chubby and plump, a right jolly old elf,
And I laughed when I saw him in spite of myself;

A wink of his eye and a twist of his head
Soon gave me to know I had nothing to dread;

He spoke not a word, but went straight to his work,
And filled all the stockings; then turned with a jerk,

And laying his finger aside of his nose,
And giving a nod, up the chimney he rose.

He sprang to his sleigh, to his team gave a whistle,
And away they all flew like the down of a thistle.

But I heard him exclaim 'ere he drove out of sight—
"Happy Christmas to all and to all a good night!"

ABOUT THE AUTHOR

CLEMENT CLARKE MOORE (1779–1863) was famously known for his real estate, having been largely responsible for the development of the Chelsea neighborhood in Manhattan. He also acted as a professor of Oriental and Greek Literature at General Theological Seminary of the Protestant Episcopal Church, a position which stopped him from publicly claiming authorship of his Christmas poem for over a decade.

A Bit of History

"'Twas the Night Before Christmas" was originally published as "Account of a Visit from St. Nicholas" in 1823 and it had an enormous impact across the United States. The poem contributed heavily to the conception of Santa Claus and gift-giving as Christmas traditions and was deemed one of the best-known verses of the nineteenth century. This popularity makes it even stranger that the authorship of the poem stayed a mystery for 15 years after its publication.

Moore eventually claimed authorship of "'Twas the Night Before Christmas" in 1837 and included it in his 1844 anthology, *Poems*. The basis for the titular character was a mixture of a nearby Dutch handyman and the historic Saint Nicholas—features of which are still associated with Santa Claus today and will make for a familiar and enjoyable reading experience.

DECK THE HALL

Traditional Welsh Carol

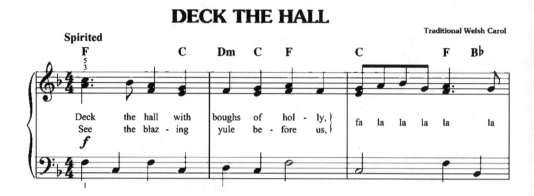

Deck the hall with boughs of hol - ly, }
See the blaz - ing yule be - fore us, } fa la la la la la

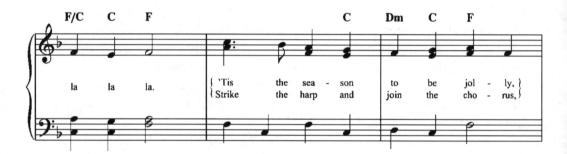

la la la. { 'Tis the sea - son to be jol - ly, }
{ Strike the harp and join the cho - rus, }

fa la la la la la la la la. { Don we now our
{ Fol - low me in

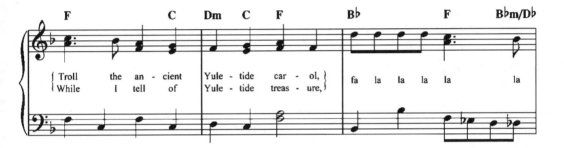

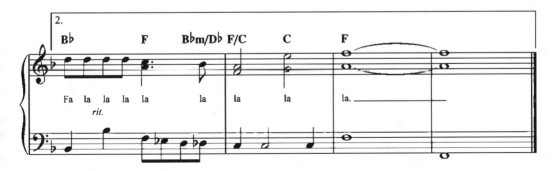

THE NUTCRACKER AND THE MOUSE KING

By Ernst T. A. Hoffmann

TRANSLATED BY LOUISE F. ENCKING

CONTENTS

THE DAY BEFORE

It was the day before Christmas. Fritz and Marie Stahlbaum sat huddled together on a sofa in a little back room, for they had been forbidden to go near the living room or the drawing room. Fritz was whispering very secretly to Marie. "Early this morning," he told her, "I heard all kinds of noises—rustling of paper and pounding behind the locked rooms." Also, he confided to her, "I saw a small, dark man, with a large box under his arm, glide noiselessly through the hall."

"Who could that have been?" asked Marie.

"Why, Godfather Drosselmeier! Who else could it have been?"

At this Marie clapped her little hands for joy, and exclaimed, "Oh, what kind of a beautiful toy can it be that Godfather has made for us this year?"

Judge Drosselmeier was not a handsome man. He was short and thin, and his face was full of wrinkles. Over his right eye he wore a large black patch and as he had lost all his hair; he wore a beautiful white wig. To be sure, the children knew that Godfather was a very skillful man, for he not only understood clocks but he also made some himself.

This was the reason that whenever one of the clocks became ill and could not sing anymore, they sent for Godfather Drosselmeier. He would come, remove his wig and his little yellow coat, and, tying on an apron, would take out a pointed instrument and run it into the clock. This always made little Marie sad, but seemed to help the clock, as it at once became alive again and began to purr, to strike and to sing, to the great joy of everyone.

Always when he came he brought something attractive in his pocket for the children. Once it was a marionette, who could curtsy and turn his eyes; once a box, out of which a bird would hop; and another time it would be a new kind of toy such as they had never seen. But when Christmas came he always made some beautiful mechanical toy which only a very clever man could make. For this reason their parents would put it away for safekeeping after it had been presented to them.

"Oh! What kind of an ingenious thing can it be that Godfather Drosselmeier has made for us this year?" whispered Marie.

"This time," replied Fritz, "it can hardly be anything else than a fortress, in which all kinds of handsome soldiers are marching back and forth. Other soldiers must come to storm the fortress, and then all at once, the soldiers inside will fire a cannon which will make a noise like thunder."

"No, no," interrupted Marie, "Godfather Drosselmeier told me about a nice garden, in which there is a large lake, on which superb swans with gold neckbands are swimming and singing lovely songs. Then a little girl comes out of the garden to the lake and beckons the swans and feeds them with candy."

"Swans do not eat candy," Fritz interrupted harshly, "and an entire garden Godfather cannot make. Then, too, we have very little joy from his toys; they are always taken away from us at once. I would rather have what Father and Mother give us, for those toys we can keep and do with as we like."

Again the children took turns in guessing what presents they were to receive this year. Marie thought that Mamsell Trudchen, her large doll, had changed much—for clumsier than ever, she was always falling to the floor. This showed in bad marks on her face, and her clothing was now anything but clean. All her warnings had not helped. And Mother had smiled to herself when she had seen how pleased Marie had been with Gretchen's little parasol. Fritz assured Marie that he was much in need of a fine chestnut horse to add to his stable, and he also needed to add cavalry to his troops. He declared Father was well aware of this. Little Marie became quiet as if in meditation, but Fritz murmured to himself, "A chestnut horse and hussars I should love to have."

In the meantime, it had become very dark. Fritz and Marie, sitting close together, did not dare to speak. It seemed to them they could hear the rustling of wings and from a far distance superb music. A bright light now appeared upon the wall and the children knew that the Christ Child had gone on to other happy children.

In that moment they heard a silvery bell ring ting-a-ling, ting-a-ling, and the doors flew open and such a splendor greeted them from these rooms that both children exclaimed, "Oh! Oh!" and stood entranced on the threshold. Then Father and Mother came forward, took the children by the hand, and said, "Come, come, dear children and see what the Christ Child has brought for you."

THE GIFTS

One can just imagine how the children stood and stared, quite silently, and how after some little time Marie, with a deep sigh, called, "Oh how beautiful—how beautiful," and Fritz turned several somersaults successfully. The children must have been very good and obedient throughout the year, for never before had they received such superb presents.

The large Christmas tree in the center was laden with gold and silver apples, and like birds and blossoms, sugar almonds, and bright bonbons, and other pretty cakes came forth from the branches. The most wonderful thing about the tree, however, was the hundreds of lights that sparkled like stars, and the tree seemed to invite them in a most friendly fashion to come and pluck its buds and fruits. Around the tree everything shone in bright and superb colors.

What beautiful things there were—yes, almost impossible to describe. Marie at once noticed the neatest, daintiest dolls and all kinds of little utensils. A silk dress, trimmed with colorful ribbons, was hanging on a rack so that Marie could look at it from all sides, and this she did, and kept calling, "Oh, the beautiful, dear dress! And shall I really be allowed to wear it?"

In the meantime Fritz had galloped three or four times around the table on his new chestnut horse, which he had really found hitched to the table. Dismounting, he announced that it was a wild horse but he would soon tame him. Then he noticed his new squadron of hussars which were very splendidly dressed in red and gold uniforms, carried silver weapons, and rode on such shimmering white horses that one could almost believe they too were of silver.

Just as the children had quieted down a little, they espied open picture books and were looking at them when the bell rang again. They now knew that Godfather Drosselmeier would present his gifts, and hurried to the table near the wall. The screen behind which he had been hiding such a long time was quickly removed. And what may we suppose they saw?

On a green lawn with many bright flowers stood a large castle that had mirror windows and gold towers.

A chime of bells could be heard ringing. Doors and windows flew open and they saw tiny men and women richly adorned with plumed hats and long, trained robes promenading in the rooms. The central hall almost seemed to be in flames, because so many little lights were burning in silver candelabra. Little children in short waistcoats and skirts were dancing, keeping time with the chimes. A gentleman in an emerald-green cloak beckoned from one of the windows and then disappeared again, and yes, even Godfather Drosselmeier, no higher than father's thumb, would appear at the door of the castle and then go back into it again.

Fritz, with his arms resting on the table, had been looking at the castle, and the dancing, and promenading little figures when he called, "Godfather Drosselmeier, let me go into your castle."

The judge explained to him that this was impossible. He was right, for it was stupid of Fritz to think he could go into a castle which even with its gold towers was so much smaller than himself. Of course Fritz could understand this, but after a while, when in the same manner the ladies and gentlemen promenaded, the children danced, the green-cloaked man appeared at the window, and Godfather Drosselmeier came to the door over and over again, Fritz called impatiently, "Godfather Drosselmeier, now you must come out of the other door."

"That cannot be done," the judge replied.

"Well, then make the green man who looks out of the window walk with the others."

"No, that cannot be brought about either," replied the judge.

"Well," cried Fritz, "then let the children come out, so I can examine them better."

The judge became vexed, and replied impatiently, "As the mechanism is made, so it must remain."

"Well," said Fritz in a subdued tone, "then I prefer my hussars. They can be made to maneuver forward and backward the way I want them to and are not locked up in a house."

Then he ran to the other table and had his squadron on the silver horses march back and forth and perform to his heart's content.

Marie also had slipped away, for she, too, had tired of seeing the dolls in the castle always doing the same thing, but being more polite than Fritz she did not wish anyone to notice it. The judge had become cheerful again and gave the children some handsome brown men and women, with gold faces, hands, and legs. These smelled sweet and delicious like honey cakes, which was a pleasant surprise.

THE SURPRISE

Marie had not left the Christmas table for she had just discovered something she had not noticed before. When Fritz had removed his soldiers who had been "on parade" just next to the tree, a splendid little man became visible, standing there quietly and modestly.

To be sure, much fault could be found with his body, for the trunk not only seemed much too large for the thin little legs, but the head also seemed too large. His clothes, however, covered up his defects, as these seemed to belong to a man of taste and culture. He was dressed in a glossy violet coat worn by hussars, with many white buttons and lacings, the same kind of trousers, and the handsomest little boots that ever were seen on the feet of an officer. These fitted the neat little legs so closely that they seemed to be painted on them.

It was comical that with this outfit he should have worn a narrow, clumsy cape that looked quite wooden, and on his head a miner's cap. Marie in noticing this remembered that Godfather Drosselmeier also wore a very plain cloak and a funny cap, but still was a very dear godfather.

While Marie was examining this neat little man more intently, for she had taken a fancy to him at her first glance, she became more and more aware of what a good-natured expression his face had. From his light green eyes, a little too large and protruding, nothing but friendship and good will shone forth. Around his chin the little man wore a most becoming, well-cared-for beard of white cotton, which made more noticeable the jolly smile on his lips.

"Oh, Father," Marie called suddenly, "to whom does the darling little man belong, who is leaning against the tree?"

"That little man," replied the father, "shall work industriously for all of you. He shall crack all the hard nuts for you with his teeth, and he belongs as much to your older sister Luise as to you and Fritz."

With that their father picked him up carefully from the table and when he lifted up the wooden cape the little man opened his mouth very wide, showing two rows of very white, pointed teeth. Marie, at her father's request, pushed a nut into his mouth, and crack—the little man had bitten it to pieces, so that the shell fell away and the sweet kernel of the nut remained in her hands.

Now everyone knew at once, even Marie, that this dainty little man was a descendant of the race of nutcrackers and was carrying on the business of his forefathers.

Marie cried out with joy, and her father said, "As you, Marie, are so much pleased with your friend Mr. Nutcracker, he shall be under your care and protection. Sister Luise and Fritz, however, shall have as much right to use him as you have."

Marie embraced the Nutcracker at once and had him crack some nuts, but she always chose the smallest so that the little man did not need to open his mouth too wide, for that was not becoming to him. Luise, too, came over, and for her also Mr. Nutcracker had to do service, which, however, he seemed to enjoy, as he kept right on smiling.

Fritz, in the meantime, had become tired from so much riding and exercising. When he heard the merry cracking of nuts, he jumped up and joined his sisters. He was laughing heartily at the sight of the comical little man, who was being passed from hand to hand and could not stop opening and closing his mouth with a snap. Fritz kept pushing the largest and hardest nuts into the Nutcracker's mouth until all of a sudden—crack, crack—three little teeth fell out of his mouth and his whole lower jaw was loose and shaky.

"Oh my poor, dear Nutcracker," sobbed Marie and took him away from Fritz.

"He is a foolish, stupid fellow," said Fritz. "He wants to be a Nutcracker and has a weak set of teeth—and probably doesn't understand his trade either. Give him to me, Marie. He shall crack nuts for me even if he loses the rest of his teeth and all of his jaw, for who cares for that good-for-nothing!"

"No, no," replied Marie, "you shall not have my dear Nutcracker—just see how sadly he is looking at me and showing me his sore mouth. You, you are a hard-hearted person—you whip your horses and perhaps you would even have one of your soldiers punished with death."

"That must be, has to be, you don't understand," called Fritz, "but the Nutcracker belongs as much to me as to you, so give him to me."

Marie began to cry violently and quickly wrapped the sick Nutcracker in her little handkerchief.

The parents came forward with Godfather Drosselmeier. "I have expressly placed the Nutcracker under Marie's protection," said the father, "and as I see that he needs it very much at this time, she shall have full power, without anyone else having anything to say about it. I am much astonished at Fritz, that he should require further service from someone who became ill while serving him. He ought to know that one never places a wounded soldier in rank and file."

Fritz was much ashamed, and without paying any more attention to nuts or Nutcracker, crept over to the other side of the table where his hussars, after posting strong sentinels on guard, had moved into their night quarters.

Marie gathered up Nutcracker's lost teeth, and around his injured chin she tied a pretty white ribbon which she had unfastened from her dress. Then she wrapped him even more carefully into her handkerchief as he seemed to look pale and frightened. Thus she rocked him in her arms, as if he were a small child, and looked at the beautiful pictures in the new picture book which was among the many other gifts received today.

MAGIC

In the Stahlbaums' living room, just as one entered the door, on the left wall stood a high cupboard in which the children kept all the pretty things which were given to them each year. Their father had this cupboard made by a very skillful cabinetmaker, who had used such clear glass and had arranged everything in it so cleverly that all the gifts looked brighter and lovelier in it than when one held them in one's hands.

On the upper shelf, inaccessible to Marie and Fritz, stood Godfather Drosselmeier's mechanical toys and the shelf just below it contained their picture books. The two lower shelves Fritz and Marie used for whatever they wanted. It usually happened, however, that Marie used the lower space as a home for her dolls, while Fritz used the shelf above it as barracks for his soldiers.

That was what had happened today also, for while Fritz was setting up his hussars above, Marie had taken out Mamsell Trudchen, and had moved the new, beautifully dressed doll into the well-furnished rooms and had invited herself to tea and cakes. The room was certainly well furnished, and any other child would have been happy to possess such a little flowered sofa, such charming little chairs, such a dear tea table, and above all, such a bright brass bed in which the most beautiful dolls could rest. All of this stood in the corner of the cupboard, the walls of which were papered with gay colored pictures. In this room, the new doll, whose name was Mamsell Clarchen, could feel much at home.

It was almost midnight and Godfather Drosselmeier had been gone for a long time, and still Fritz and Marie could not come away from the cupboard, although their mother was urging them to go to bed.

"It is true," called Fritz, "the poor hussars also want to rest, for while I am here not one even dares to nod, I am certain of that."

With that he departed, but Marie was begging, "Just a little while longer; let me stay here, Mother, as I have several things to attend to; and when they are done, I will go to bed at once."

As Marie was a sensible and obedient child her mother could leave her with the playthings without worrying about her. To guard against her being so engrossed in the new doll that she might forget the lights, her mother extinguished all those around the cupboard, and left burning only the lamp that was suspended from the ceiling in the middle of the room, which gave a soft mellow light.

"Go to bed soon, dear, or you will not be able to get up in time tomorrow morning," called her mother, as she went into her bedroom.

As soon as Marie found she was alone, she began to do the things so dear to her heart. She still had the injured Nutcracker in her arm, wrapped in her handkerchief, and now she laid him carefully on the table, unwrapped him and looked after his wounds. Nutcracker was very pale, and smiled so sadly that Marie became sad herself.

"Oh, Nutcracker," she whispered, "do not be angry that brother Fritz hurt you so. He did not mean to do it, but he has become a little hard-hearted through his being so much with rough soldiers. But aside from this he is a very good boy, I can assure you. Now I will nurse you until you are well and happy again. I shall ask Godfather Drosselmeier to replace your teeth and set your shoulder, as he understands how to do such things."

When she pronounced the name of Drosselmeier, she noticed that her friend, the Nutcracker, drew down his mouth, and his eyes seemed to spout green sparks. Just as she was about to be surprised, however, she noticed the Nutcracker had the same honest face again, with the same sad smile, and she concluded it must have been the draft that made the lamp flicker which had so changed his face. "Am I not a foolish girl to be so easily frightened and to believe that this wooden doll could make up faces? But I do love the Nutcracker because he is so comical and good-natured, and for that reason he must be nursed."

Then Marie took Mr. Nutcracker in her arms, walked over to the cupboard, and stooping down whispered to the new doll, "I beg of you, dear Mamsell Clarchen, be generous and give your bed to the ill and wounded Nutcracker, and make use of the sofa, as best you can. Remember that you are well and strong, for otherwise you would not have such fat, red cheeks. Remember, too, that very few of the most beautiful dolls possess such a soft sofa."

Clarchen, in her splendid Christmas apparel, looked very elegant and selfish, but uttered no word.

"Why do I go to so much trouble?" said Marie, placing the Nutcracker quietly and softly in the bed and, taking a ribbon she had worn, she put it around his wounded shoulders and covered him up almost to his nose. "But he must not remain near Clarchen," she said, and took the bed with the Nutcracker in it and placed it in the upper shelf, right near the village where Fritz's hussars were encamped.

She locked the cupboard and was going into the bedroom when she heard a soft rustling, fluttering, and whispering behind the stove, behind the chairs, and behind the cabinet. The tall grandfather's pendulum clock whirred louder and louder, but it did not strike. Marie looked up and saw that the large, gilded owl sitting on the clock had lowered her wings so that the whole top of the clock was covered, and the ugly cathead with the crooked bill was pushed forward.

And louder it bussed, with distinct words:

"Tick-tock, tick-tock—softly purrs the clock.

Little Mouse King's ears can hear,

Whirr, whirr, whirr.

Sing him the songs of yore

For soon he'll be no more.

Strike, clock, strike!"

And pum, pum, pum, it struck with a muffled and hollow sound twelve times. Marie, now badly scared, was about to run away when she saw Godfather Drosselmeier sitting on the clock instead of the owl, with his yellow coat-tails like wings hanging down on either side.

She called in a crying voice, "Godfather Drosselmeier, Godfather Drosselmeier, what are you doing up there? Come on down and do not frighten me so, you bad godfather."

Just then a furious giggling and whistling started all around her and it seemed to her as if a thousand little feet were trotting and running in the walls, and a thousand little lights were looking through the cracks in the floor. But they were not lights. No, no, they were sparkling little eyes and Marie became aware that everywhere mice were peeping out and were pushing themselves forward.

Very soon she heard trot, trot, trot, hop, hop, hop, and more and more mice galloped around and at last took positions in distinct rows, just as Fritz's soldiers did when they were ready to go into battle. Marie thought this very funny, and, as she was not afraid of mice, her timidity left her. Then, all at once, she heard such a shrill whistle that the chills ran down her back.

Now, what do you suppose she saw? Just in front of her feet, as if it had come through the floor, there appeared with a hissing and whistling noise a mouse with seven heads, a bright crown glistening on each head. The mouse with its seven heads and seven crowns gave three loud squeaks, which seemed to be a command to the entire regiment, for they moved forward at once. Then trot, trot, trot, hop, hop, hop, they came toward the cupboard and directly toward Marie, who was standing close to the glass door.

Her heart was beating so fast from being afraid that she felt as if it would jump out. Half fainting, she turned, when clash, clash, and the pane of glass from the cabinet fell to the floor, for Marie had pushed her elbow through it. At that moment she felt a sharp pain in her left arm, but forgot it for the moment in her relief at hearing no more hissing and squeaking. Everything had quieted down, and although she did not dare look toward the floor, she thought the clatter of the falling glass must have frightened the mice into their holes.

But what did she hear now? Just behind her in the cabinet there was a commotion, and low, pleasant voices said, "Wake up, wake up; we must fight, we must fight; in this night, in this night," and accompanying these voices she could hear a chime of bells ring out merrily.

"Oh!" said Marie, "those are my little chimes." As she moved to one side, she saw strange lights and caught glimpses of all the dolls running around waving their arms excitedly.

All at once Mr. Nutcracker arose, threw the blanket away and jumped out of bed with both feet at once, calling loudly, "Crack-crack-crack, foolish mouse pack, crick-crack, crick-crack!"

With that he pulled out his little sword and flourished it in the air, calling, "You, my dear vassals, friends, and brothers, will you assist me in this severe combat?"

At once three marionettes, one pantalon, four chimney sweeps, two zither players, and one drum major called out, "Yes sir, we will cleave to you most loyally. We will go forward with you to combat, victory or death," and followed the enthusiastic Nutcracker in a dangerous leap from the second shelf. Yes, they could easily follow, for not only did they wear clothes of silk and velvet, but inside they were made of cotton and sawdust, and fell down like bags of wool.

But the poor Nutcracker would certainly break his arms and legs, for it was almost two feet from the upper to the lower shelf and his body was as brittle as if it had been blown of glass. Yes, Nutcracker would certainly have broken his arms and legs, if at the instant he was about to jump Mamsell Clarchen had not leaped from the sofa and caught the hero, sword and all, in her two arms.

Quickly he tore off the ribbon with which Marie had tied up his shoulder, pressed it to his lips, and using it for a sash, swung his bright sword boldly and jumped like a bird from the edge of the cabinet to the floor. At this moment one could hear the squeaking and screeching of the mice again. Oh, under the large table was the army of mice, and above all towered the bad Mouse King with the seven heads. Oh, now what will happen!

THE BATTLE OF THE SUGAR BULLETS

"Beat the general march, trusty drummer," called the Nutcracker.

Very loudly and at once the drummer began to drum in the most artistic manner, so that the windows in the glass cabinet shook and rumbled. Now it began to roar and rattle inside. Marie became aware that the covers of the boxes in which Fritz's army was encamped had opened and the soldiers jumped down into the lower shelf, and there formed into a battalion.

Nutcracker ran toward Pantalon, who, pale and with chin quivering, said very solemnly, "General, I know your courage and your experience and now we must consider the whole situation and make a quick decision. I entrust you with the command of the several cavalry and artillery companies. A horse you do not need for you have long legs and can gallop fairly well. Do now what your profession demands."

Pantalon immediately pressed his long thin fingers to his mouth and gave such a sharp whistle that it sounded as if a hundred little trumpets were blown.

Then one could hear stamping and neighing in the cabinet, and Fritz's cuirassiers and dragoons came forward, the new hussars foremost.

All took their positions on the floor. Now regiment after regiment marched past Nutcracker with flying colors and martial music and stood at attention across the floor of the room. Before them all rattled Fritz's cannon, surrounded by the gunners. In a few moments one could hear them boom, and soon Marie saw the sugar bullets playing havoc among the mice. Especially noticeable and shooting from Mother's footstool was a battery which shot honey cakes into the mice, scattering and bowling them over.

Still they came nearer and nearer, even running over the cannon. Then boom—boom, and Marie could hardly see what was happening for dust and smoke, but she was certain that a victory on either side was doubtful. The mice seemed to produce more troops right along, and the little silver pills which they hurled so skillfully could be heard as they struck the glass of the cabinet. Then burr, burr, puff, boom, boom, rip, rip, rap, and all the mice and the Mouse King squeaked and screeched, and above it all one could hear Nutcracker's mighty voice, giving out necessary commands, as he strode past the firing battalions.

During the heat of battle, troops of mice cavalry swarmed out from under the cabinet, and with a great fury and loud squeaking attacked the left wing of Nutcracker's army. But what resistance did they find here? Slowly, for the condition of the floor would allow no haste, one corps under the command of two Chinese emperors had pushed forward and taken position in the square. These brave, gayly colored, and lordly troops, consisting of many gardeners, Tyroleans, clowns, harlequins, barbers, lions, tigers, and monkeys were fighting with composure, courage, and persistence.

With heroic bravery this battalion would have wrested the victory from the enemy, had it not been that a daring, hostile mouse captain rashly pushed himself forward and bit off the head of a Chinese emperor, who in falling killed two Tyroleans and one monkey.

This made a break in the line through which the enemy gained entrance, and soon the entire battalion was shattered, so that Nutcracker stood before the cabinet with only a handful of men.

"The Reserves, forward! Pantalon! Tambour! Skaramuz! Where are you?" called the Nutcracker, who was hoping for more troops from the cabinet. A few dark-skinned men and women, the honey cakes with gold faces, hats, and helmets, came forward, but they fought so stupidly that they did not hit the enemy, and came near tearing the cap from their own commander-in-chief. The enemy riflemen soon bit off their legs, so they fell forward and in doing so killed several of Nutcracker's companions in arms.

Now the Nutcracker was entirely surrounded by the enemy and was in the greatest danger and distress. He wanted to jump over the ledge of the cabinet, but his legs were too short. Clara and Gretchen had fainted and so could not help him. Hussars and dragoons leaped merrily by him into the cabinet. In his great need he called, "A horse! A horse! My kingdom for a horse!" At that instant two enemies took hold of his wooden cape, and in triumph the Mouse King came forward at full speed, screeching from his seven throats.

Hardly realizing what she was doing, Marie called, "Oh, my poor Nutcracker," took off her left slipper and hurled it with all the force she could muster into the pack of mice and their Mouse King.

At this moment everything seemed to be in confusion and to float away, for the pain in Marie's left arm was more severe than before, and she sank to the floor in a faint.

THE PLEASANT SURPRISE

When Marie awoke from her deep sleep, she was lying in her bed and the bright sun shone through the ice-covered panes of the windows. Close beside her sat a strange man whom she soon recognized as Dr. Wendelstern. In a low voice he whispered, "Now she is awake." Then Marie's mother came in and looked at her with an anxious, searching glance.

"Oh! Mother dear," whispered Marie, "are all those horrid mice gone and was the good Nutcracker rescued?"

The doctor winked to her mother as she replied, "Don't worry, my child. All the mice are gone and the Nutcracker is in the cabinet safe and sound. But we have been much worried about you, for that is what happens when children are disobedient and do not mind their parents. You played with your dolls very late last evening, and you became sleepy. Perhaps a little mouse came out from under the cupboard, although we seldom see one, and frightened you. You pushed your elbow into a pane of glass in the cabinet and cut your arm so severely that the doctor just now removed little splinters of glass, and says you might have had a stiff arm, or even bled to death. Thank heaven I awoke about midnight and, seeing you were not in your bed, I went into the living room. There you were with Fritz's soldiers and your dolls all about you. The Nutcracker was on your bleeding arm and not far away was your left slipper."

"Yes, Mother," Marie interrupted, "those were still the traces of the great battle between the dolls and the mice. I became so terrified when the Nutcracker was taken prisoner that I threw my shoe at the mice and after that I don't remember what happened."

Now the doctor took her pulse and said she had better stay in bed as she had a little fever. Thus she had to remain in bed several days and the time passed very slowly for she couldn't play or do much. Only at twilight her mother would come in and sit with her and tell her lovely stories.

Just as her mother had finished the story of Prince Farkardin, the door opened and Godfather Drosselmeier entered with the words, "Well, I really wanted to come myself and see how Marie is and how her injured arm is getting on."

When Marie saw her godfather, the picture of the night before came into her mind, and she called to him, "Oh! Godfather, you were very horrid last night. I saw you sit on the clock and spread your coattails so it shouldn't strike loud and frighten the mice away. I also heard you call the Mouse King. Why didn't you come to the rescue of Nutcracker and me, for you are to blame that I am ill and wounded in bed."

Marie's mother asked in an anxious tone, "Why, what is the matter, Marie?"

Godfather, however, made up faces and said in a snarling voice,

"Strike clock, strike,

Pendulum goes click-clock—

Hink and honk and honk and hink—

Tick-tock, tick-tock."

Marie looked at Godfather Drosselmeier with staring eyes, for he looked uglier than ever, swinging his right arm backward and forward as if he were a marionette. She might have been afraid of Godfather if her mother had not been present and if Fritz, who had sneaked in, had not interrupted with loud laughing, "Oh, you are too comical today. You remind me of my jack-in-the-box. I grew tired of him and threw him behind the stove."

Marie's mother remained serious and asked the judge what he meant by such antics. The judge laughingly replied, "Have you entirely forgotten my clock song? I always sing it to patients like Marie." With this he sat down close to Marie's bed and said, "Do not be angry with me that I didn't at once put out the fourteen eyes of the Mouse King. It couldn't be done. Instead I will give you a pleasant surprise." With these words he reached into his pocket and slowly pulled out the Nutcracker whose teeth and jaw he had set back into place.

Marie chuckled for joy, but her mother smiled and said, "Now do you see how much Godfather Drosselmeier thinks of your Nutcracker?"

"You must confess, however," the judge interrupted Mrs. Stahlbaum, "that the Nutcracker's body could be improved upon and that his face can hardly be called handsome. How such a lack of beauty came into his family and was handed down from one generation to another I will tell you, if you wish to hear the story. Perhaps Marie knows the story of Princess Pirlipat, the witch Mouserinks and the skillful watchmaker?"

"Listen to me," called Fritz at this instant. "Godfather Drosselmeier, you really inserted the teeth of the Nutcracker and his jaw isn't as shaky as it was either, but why has he no sword; why didn't you fasten one to his belt?"

"Oh!" replied the judge rather impatiently, "you always have to find fault and criticize, boy! What concern of mine is Nutcracker's sword? I have cured his body, he can himself see where he finds a sword."

"That is true," replied Fritz, "if he amounts to anything he will see to it that he gets some weapons."

"Well, Marie," the judge continued, "tell me, do you know the story of the Princess Pirlipat?"

"No, I don't," replied Marie, "do tell it, will you please?"

"I hope, Judge," said Mrs. Stahlbaum, "that your story will not be as full of scares as those you usually tell."

'Indeed not, Mrs. Stahlbaum," replied the judge, "on the contrary, this story that I am about to tell is full of fun."

"Oh! Begin, begin, dear Godfather," the children called, and the judge told the story.

Fairy Tale of the Hard Nut

When he saw her lying in the cradle, Pirlipat's mother was the wife of a king, and therefore a queen, and Pirlipat herself a princess. The king was very joyful when his beautiful daughter was born. When he saw her lying in the cradle, he danced around her and called, "Oh! Has anyone ever seen a more beautiful child than my little Pirlipat?" All the members of his staff, his prime minister and his generals replied, "Never!"

It was not to be denied, for it was a fact that since the world stood there had probably been no more beautiful child than Princess Pirlipat. Her face looked as if it were woven of lily-white and faint pink silk flakes, her eyes were azure blue, her curly hair resembled gold thread. With all that, Pirlipat had brought two rows of pearly teeth with her when she came into the world.

Everyone was happy. Only the queen seemed restless and anxious, and no one knew why. It was especially noticeable that she had someone watch Pirlipat's cradle all the time. In addition to the doors being guarded by sentinels, and two nurses at the cradle, she had six nurses sitting around the room night after night. But what seemed too foolish for words, each of the six nurses was obliged to hold on her lap a cat which was to be petted all night, so it would purr continually.

It is impossible to guess why Pirlipat's mother ordered all these arrangements, but I know why and will now tell you. Once upon a time many kings and princes were gathered at the court of Pirlipat's father, and they had a brilliant entertainment. Many tournaments, comedies, and court balls were given. The king, in order to impress the court with his wealth (and wishing to make a good levy from the Crown treasury), produced an entertainment such as had seldom been seen. As he had been told by the chief steward, that the court astronomer had appointed this time for preparing meats, he ordered a huge banquet and invited all the kings and princes to a bowl of soup in order to surprise them with his feast.

Then he said very pleasantly to the queen, "You know, dear, how much I like sausage!"

The queen knew full well what he was suggesting, for it was his wish that she should oversee the preparation of this sausage. The chief steward was ordered to deliver at once the gold sausage utensils and silver casseroles to the kitchen. A large fire of sandalwood was started. The queen put on a damask apron and soon the savory odor of the sausage and soup met one's nostrils.

Even to the council chamber this smell found its way and the king out of sheer delight sprang up and, "With your permission, gentlemen," he rushed into the kitchen, embraced the queen, and stirring something into the kettle with his gold scepter, returned to the council chamber. Right now was the important moment when the pork was to be cut into little squares and fried on silver broilers. The ladies of the court withdrew, as the queen wished to do this work alone in order to show her affection and respect for the king.

But just as the pork was beginning to fry, she heard a fine, low voice whisper, "Give me some of the pork sausage, sister. I want to feast also—I too am a queen—give me some pork."

The queen knew at once that it was Mrs. Mouserinks, the Mouse Queen, who was speaking. Mrs. Mouserinks had been living in the palace many years. She declared that she was related to the royal family and that she was Queen of Mousedom and had a large household under the hearth. The queen was a good and generous woman, and while she did not wish to acknowledge Mrs. Mouserinks as queen and sister, she was glad to bestow some of the pork on this day of feasting and she replied, "Come out, Mrs. Mouserinks, and I will give you some of my pork."

Then Mrs. Mouserinks leaped merrily onto the hearth and taking the squares of pork very daintily into her little paws, ate one after the other as the queen gave them to her. But all at once Mrs. Mouserinks' aunts, uncles, and cousins came forward, as well as her seven sons, who were naughty rascals, and jumped into the pork so that the queen could not defend herself and was much frightened.

Luckily the Lord High Stewardess just then appeared and chased away the unwelcome guests, so that there was a little pork left. This the court mathematician, who was called for the purpose, divided very artfully into all of the sausages. Drums and trumpets sounded and the princes and dukes came to the feast in gala attire, some on white horses, others in crystal coaches. The king received them with the greatest cordiality and graciousness and then clad in crown and scepter, took his place as sovereign at the head of the table.

When the liver sausage was presented, however, one could see how very much disappointed the king was, for he became paler and paler. He lifted his eyes to heaven; he sighed and sighed, as if he had a severe pain. When the blood sausage came, however, he sank sobbing and crying into the back of his armchair, put both his hands before his face and moaned and lamented. Everyone rose from the table. The king's physician tried in vain to take the unhappy king's pulse, but a deep, nameless sorrow seemed to rack him. At last, after much urging, and the use of strong remedies, the king seemed to recover somewhat—and he murmured, "Not enough pork."

Then the queen came forward, threw herself at his feet and murmured, "Oh! my poor, unhappy husband, how you have suffered, but here you see the guilty one and here belongs the punishment. Oh! It was Mrs. Mouserinks with her seven sons and all her cousins and relations who ate all the pork." And then the queen fainted.

The king jumped up in rage and called, "Chief Stewardess, how did this happen?" The Chief Stewardess related all she knew and the king decided to take revenge on Mrs. Mouserinks and her family, who had robbed him of his pork. The Privy Councillor was sent for, and it was decided to institute proceedings to take possession of her estate. The king, however, was of the opinion that in the meantime she could still be eating his pork and suggested that the matter be settled by the court clockmaker. This man, whose name was the same as mine, namely, Christian Elias Drosselmeier, promised to rid the palace forever of Mrs. Mouserinks and her family through a very clever device.

He found very artful little machines in which he fastened bacon with a thread, which Mr. Drosselmeier placed all around the residence of Mrs. Bacon-eater. But Mrs. Mouserinks was much too wise not to see her danger in this plan. In spite of all her warning and pleading, not being able to resist the sweet smell of the fried bacon, her seven sons, as well as many of her relatives, went into the little machines. Just when they were beginning to nibble at the bacon, they were caught in a little wire prison, and taken to the kitchen to be cruelly executed. Mrs. Mouserinks left this region of horror with her little retinue. Sorrow, despair, and revenge filled her breast.

The Court was overjoyed, but the queen was greatly troubled, for she knew the disposition of Mrs. Mouserinks, and knew that she would have revenge for the death of her sons and her relatives. In fact, just when the queen was preparing a special dish for the king, Mrs. Mouserinks appeared to the queen and said:

"My sons, my cousins and my relatives have all been killed. Be careful, Madame Queen, that the Mouse Queen does not bite your little princess to pieces. Be very careful." The queen became so terror-stricken that she burned the favorite dish she was preparing for the king, thus for a second time making the king angry. But this is all of the story tonight, next time more.

No matter how much Marie, who had her own ideas about the story, begged him to continue, Godfather Drosselmeier would not be persuaded to continue, but arising said, "Too much of anything is poor policy. Tomorrow we will continue."

Just as he was passing through the door Fritz called, "Tell me, Godfather, is it really true that you invented the mousetraps?"

"Why do you ask such foolish questions," called his mother, but the judge smiled and replied, "Am I not a skillful watchmaker and could I not then invent a mousetrap?"

CONTINUATION OF
THE FAIRY TALE OF THE HARD NUT

"Now you know full well, children," continued the judge the next evening, "why the queen was guarding the beautiful Princess Pirlipat so carefully."

Must she not live in constant fear that Mrs. Mouserinks would carry out her threat and return and bite the Princess so she would die? Drosselmeier's traps were of no use against the wise and crafty Mrs. Mouserinks. The astronomer of the court, who was also astrologer and reader of stars, advised that only the family of Tom Cat Purr was capable of keeping Mrs. Mouserinks away from the cradle. So it was ordered that each of the nurses should hold on her lap a son of this family, and by petting and stroking him, lighten his labors and make his services more bearable.

But once upon a time, when it was already midnight, one of the head nurses, who sat close to the cradle, suddenly awoke from a deep sleep. Around her everyone seemed to be in deep slumber, no purring, only a dead silence. But what do you suppose the head nurse saw? Right in front of her was a very ugly mouse standing on her hind feet and with her head reclining on the face of the princess.

With a cry of fright, the head nurse jumped up, everybody was alert in a moment, but in that instant Mrs. Mouserinks, for the large mouse in the cradle of little Pirlipat was no one else, ran to the corner of the room. All the counsellors plunged after her, but too late—she had disappeared through a crack in the floor. Pirlipat awoke at the noise and began to cry most dolefully.

"Thank heaven," cried the nurses, "she is alive." But how great was their sorrow when they looked at the princess and saw how the beautiful child had been changed. Instead of the golden-haired, white-and-pink little cherub face, they saw a small, thick head on a misshapen, twisted body. The azure-blue eyes had been altered to green protruding and staring ones, and her little mouth now extended from ear to ear. The queen was beside herself with misery and distress, and the walls of the king's study had to be padded, for he ran his head again and again against the wall and cried in a most distressed voice, "Oh! What an unhappy father am I."

Now he could realize that it would have been better to have eaten the sausage without the pork and to have paid no attention to Mrs. Mouserinks and her tribe under the hearth. But he placed all the blame on the court clockmaker, Christian Elias Drosselmeier of Nuremberg. For that reason he gave command that if Drosselmeier could not, within four weeks, restore the princess to her former condition, or at least find a way in which this could be accomplished, he would have him put to death by the disgraceful way of the executioner's axe.

Drosselmeier, though much alarmed, sought aid in his art and his good fortune, and began his first operation, which he deemed most necessary. He took the princess all apart, unscrewed her hands and feet, and viewed the inner structure of her body, and there to his sorrow he found that the older little Pirlipat would become, the more ungainly she would appear. Now he was at his wits' end, for what to do he did not know. He very carefully put the princess together again and sank down heartsick near her cradle, which he had been forbidden to leave.

Four weeks had already gone by—yes, it was Wednesday, when the king, with angry eyes, looked into the room and proclaimed threateningly, waving his scepter:

"Christian Elias Drosselmeier, if you do not find a remedy for the princess, you must die."

Drosselmeier wept bitterly, but Princess Pirlipat very contentedly cracked nuts. It was the first time that the clockmaker had noted Pirlipat's unusual appetite for nuts, and in particular he noted the teeth with which she had been born. In fact, directly after her change she had cried incessantly until a nut was given to her. This she cracked, ate the kernel of it and then became quiet.

"Oh, wise sign of nature," cried Christian Elias, "you show me the gate to this secret—I will knock, and you will open." He at once begged permission to have an interview with the court astronomer, and was led to him in care of his guards.

Both men embraced with tears in their eyes, as they had become firm friends. They entered a private room and began to read book after book, dealing with many mysteries. Night overtook them and the court astronomer looked at the stars, and began with the help of Mr. Drosselmeier, who also understood the art, to cast the horoscope of Princess Pirlipat. It was most difficult, but at last—what joy—it was clearly to be seen, that in order to break the spell of the enchantment which had made her so ugly and deformed and bring back her former beauty, it was only necessary that she should eat the sweet kernel of a Krakatuk nut.

A Krakatuk nut has such a hard shell that a forty-pound-weight cannon could drive over it without cracking it. This hard nut must be cracked by a man, who had never been shaved, and who had never worn boots. He must do this in the presence of the princess and he must pass the nut to her with closed eyes. Only after he had gone backwards seven steps, without stumbling, was he allowed to open his eyes.

Three days and three nights these men had worked without ceasing, and the king was at his dinner on Saturday when Drosselmeier, who was to have been beheaded on Sunday morning, entered full of joy and loud rejoicing and told of the remedy they had discovered which would bring back the lost beauty of the princess. The king joyfully embraced him and promised him a sword set with diamonds, four medals, and two new Sunday coats.

"Immediately after dinner we will begin," the king stated in a very friendly way. "You must be certain, my friend, that the young man who has never shaved and never worn boots, will be at hand with the nut Krakatuk. Do not let him have any wine beforehand, so he will not stumble when he walks backward like a crab, for he can have all he wants afterwards."

Drosselmeier was much confused at the speech of the king. With fear and trembling, he informed the king that while the remedy had been found, it was now necessary to find the nut Krakatuk, as well as the young man who would crack it with his teeth, and that there was some doubt whether nut and nutcracker could be found.

"Then the order that you are to be beheaded will stand," roared the king and swung his scepter over his head. It was fortunate that the king had just partaken of a delicious dinner and was in a good humor, and therefore ready to listen to the entreaties of the queen in Drosselmeier's behalf. She took courage to inform the king that Drosselmeier's problem had been to find the remedy, and that he had accomplished this. The king said he called this quibbling, but at last concluded that the clockmaker and astronomer were to go forth at once and return with the nut Krakatuk their possession. The man to crack the nut was to procured by advertising in various papers, both at home and abroad.

Here the judge refused to go on with the story but promised to conclude it the next evening.

Conclusion of
the Fairy Tale of the Hard Nut

The next evening, as soon as the candles had been lighted, the judge continued his story.

The clockmaker and astronomer had been away fifteen years without finding a trace of the nut Krakatuk. Where they had been and what curious things had happened to them, I could talk about for weeks, but I shall not do so. I shall state at once that Drosselmeier in his sorrow now had a great longing to return to his native city of Nuremberg. This longing came over him when he and his friend were in a deep jungle in Asia, smoking a good pipe of tobacco.

"O my beautiful, beautiful native city of Nuremberg, beautiful city. He who has not seen you, even if he has traveled far and seen London, Paris, and Vienna, he must still be longing for you—for you, O Nuremberg, beautiful city, with your beautiful houses and windows."

When Drosselmeier was complaining thus bitterly, the astronomer became very sympathetic and he cried so pitifully that he could be heard from one corner of Asia to the other. But he soon composed himself, dried his tears and asked, "Why, my very esteemed comrade, do we sit here and weep? Why do we not go to Nuremberg, for is it not immaterial where and how we find this Krakatuk nut?"

"Yes, you are right," replied Drosselmeier, much comforted. Soon both of them stood up, knocked the ashes from their pipes, and went in one straight line out of the jungle in the center of Asia to Nuremberg. Soon after their arrival, Drosselmeier called on his cousin, the doll manufacturer, enameler and gilder, Christoph Zacharias Drosselmeier, whom he had not seen for many, many years. To him he told the entire story of Princess Pirlipat, of Mrs. Mouserinks and the nut Krakatuk.

The doll carver threw up his hands again and again in great astonishment and called out, "Oh cousin, cousin, what wonderful things you are telling." Drosselmeier related his adventures on his far journey, how he had lived two years with the Date King, how insolently the Almond Count had refused to see him, how he had, without success, applied for help to the Society for the Study of Natural Philosophy—in short, how all his efforts had ended in failure, and he had not even found a trace of the nut Krakatuk.

While he was telling the story, Christoph Zacharias snapped his fingers several times, turned around on one foot, held his breath and cried, "Yes, yes, unless I am much mistaken, I have it." With this he threw his hat and his wig into the air for joy, and exclaimed, "Cousin, cousin, you are saved, for I am quite certain I myself own this Krakatuk nut." Thereupon he brought out a box, from which he took a gold nut of average size.

"See," he said, showing the nut to his cousin, "this nut has a peculiar history. Many years ago, at Christmas time, a strange man appeared, with a bag of nuts which he desired to sell. Just in front of my doll booth he placed his bag on the street in order to defend himself from the blows of the native nutseller who was trying to drive him out. In that moment a heavily loaded wagon drove over the bag, cracking all the nuts except one. This nut the stranger, smiling mysteriously, offered to sell me for a dollar of the mint of 1720. I thought this rather queer, but finding such a piece of money in my pocket, I bought the nut and gilded it, not knowing really why I had paid so much for it."

There was no doubt about the cousin's nut being the long-sought Krakatuk nut, especially when the court astronomer, who had been called, scraped the gold from the nut, and there found the name carved in the shell in Chinese letters. The joy of the travelers was unbounded and the cousin was the happiest man under the sun. Drosselmeier assured him that his fortune was made, for in addition to a pension, he would see to it that he would in the future receive free of charge all the gold he needed for gilding.

The travelers had already donned their night caps and were going to bed when the astronomer said, "My dear comrade, luck never comes singly, and I believe that we have not only found the nut Krakatuk, but also the young man who shall crack it with his teeth and present the beautifying kernel to the princess. I mean, the son of your cousin. No, I cannot sleep," he continued, much excited, "but shall at once, this night, cast the young man's horoscope." With that he removed his night cap and at once began his search.

The cousin's son was, to be sure, a tall, well-built young man who had never been shaved and never worn boots. It was true that for several years during Christmas time he had been a puppet, but no one would have been able to detect this in the least. He had been educated through his father's efforts. At Christmas time he wore a handsome red coat with gold braid, carried a sword, his hat under his arm and had his hair dressed after the latest fashion with a hair net. Thus, he appeared very handsome in his father's booth and cracked nuts for the young girls. That is why they called him "Little Nutcracker."

The next morning, the astronomer embraced his friend and called with joy, "He is the one. We have found him, only we must pay attention to two things. First and foremost, you must prepare for your admirable nephew a stout wooden braid of hair which is so connected with the lower jaw that he can receive a sharp jerk with it. Secondly, we must keep it a secret in the town, that we have brought the young man with us who can crack the Krakatuk nut; in fact, it must appear as if he arrived much later. I am reading in the horoscope that if a number of men break their teeth in trying to crack the nut without success, the king will give as a reward to the young man who succeeds and thus restores her, the princess herself in marriage; and will name the young man as his successor.

The doll carver was highly pleased with the idea that his son should marry the Princess Pirlipat and become prince and king, and therefore gave the matter entirely into the keeping of the travelers. The braid of hair which Drosselmeier had very successfully attached to the promising young nephew, was working admirably, as with it he had been able to crack with his teeth any number of the hardest peach stones.

As Drosselmeier and the astronomer had at once reported the finding of the nut to the Court, all preparations for their reception were made. When the travelers arrived with the beauty restorer, many handsome young men, among them several princes, were at hand, willing to try their good set of teeth in an attempt to disenchant the princess. The travelers were much shocked when they again saw the princess. Her little body, with the tiny hands and feet, could hardly carry the deformed head. The ugliness of the face was increased by a white cotton beard which had grown around her mouth and chin.

Everything happened as the astronomer had read in the horoscope. One foolish prince after another broke his teeth and hurt his jaw, without being able to help the princess in the least, and when one, nearly fainting, was handed to a dentist, he murmured, "That was a hard nut."

After the king, in the anguish of his heart, had offered the princess, as well as his kingdom, to the one who succeeded in disenchanting the princess, the well-behaved, gentle, young Drosselmeier presented himself at court and requested that he be allowed to try his luck. After greeting the king and queen, and especially the Princess Pirlipat most politely, he received from the hands of the chief toastmaster the nut Krakatuk. He put it at once into his mouth, gave a jerk to his braid and crack, crack. The shell of the nut broke into many pieces. He very cleverly cleaned the nut from the fiber which surrounded it and with a very low curtsy handed it to the princess, after which he closed his eyes and walked backwards. The princess swallowed the nut at once, and Oh! Such a miracle! Gone was the deformity—and in her place stood a beautiful angelic young girl, with a face like peaches and cream, and azure eyes. Her curly hair looked as if it were gold thread. Trumpets and kettle drums could be heard amid the shouts of joy of the people. The king and his entire court were hopping and dancing, just as they did when Pirlipat was born, and the queen had to be restored with eau-de-cologne for she had fainted from joy and delight. The great rioting and noise confused young Drosselmeier, who had not completed his seven steps. But he bravely continued and was just putting back his right foot for the seventh step when squeaking and whining Mrs. Mouserinks arose through the floor.

The young man who was about to put his foot down stepped upon her and, stumbling, almost fell down. Oh, misfortune! All at once the young man was just as deformed as the Princess Pirlipat had been. The body was shrunken and could hardly support the large, misshapen head with its protruding eyes and its broad, gaping mouth. Instead of his braid of hair he wore a narrow wooden cape, which controlled the lower jaw.

The clockmaker and astronomer were afraid something might happen to them when they saw Mrs. Mouserinks injured on the floor. But her wickedness was not to remain unpunished, for young Mr. Drosselmeier had stepped on her neck so severely with the sharp heel of his shoes, that she was mortally wounded. When Mrs. Mouserinks was about to die, she squeaked out:

"O Krakatuk, hard nut—

From which I now must die,

Nutcracker soon will pass away.

My son with the seven crowns will repay.

And avenge his mother.

O life so full of joy, from you I must depart.

Oh, peril of death—Squeafy."

With this cry Mrs. Mouserinks departed this life and was taken away by the king's official stove tender.

No one had paid attention to young Mr. Drosselmeier, but the princess reminded the king of his promise, and he at once gave orders to have the young hero appear on the scene. When, however, the unfortunate man with his deformity stepped forward, the princess covered both her eyes and said, "Away, away with that ugly Nutcracker," and soon the court marshal took hold of him by his little shoulders and pushed him through the door. The king was furious, that he should have been expected to have a Nutcracker for a son. He blamed it all upon the stupidity of the clockmaker and astronomer and had them expelled from the court.

The horoscope which the astronomer had cast in Nuremberg had not shown this, but he was determined to seek further happenings in the stars, and here he claimed to find that the young Drosselmeier would behave so well in his new environment that in spite of his deformity, he would become prince and king. His misshapen body could disappear only when the seven-headed son of Mrs. Mouserinks, who was now the Mouse King, should be killed by him, and when a lady should love him in spite of his deformity.

We are told that it came to pass that young Drosselmeier was seen at Christmas time in his father's booth, as Nutcracker, but also was seen as a prince.

That is the fairy tale of the hard nut, and now you know why so many people say, "That was a hard nut to crack, and why Nutcrackers are usually so ugly."

And thus the judge closed his story. Marie thought that the Princess Pirlipat was unkind and grateful but Fritz assured her that if the Nutcracker was as brave as he pretended to be, he would conquer the Mouse King and thus soon regain his former fine figure.

In a week's time Marie was well again and could dance around the room as usual. In the cabinet everything looked beautiful. New, glistening trees, flowers, houses, as well as shining dolls, stood there. First of all Marie again found her beloved Nutcracker who was smiling at her from the second shelf with perfectly sound teeth. As she was looking at her favorite with great joy, she became frightened, for she remembered the story that Godfather Drosselmeier had told about the Nutcracker and the quarrel with Mrs. Mouserinks and her son. She was now satisfied that her Nutcracker could be no one else than the young Mr. Drosselmeier from Nuremberg, the very pleasant nephew of her godfather, who alas, had been bewitched by Mrs. Mouserinks. There was no doubt about it that the skilled watchmaker at the Court of Pirlipat's father was no one else than Judge Drosselmeier himself; in fact, she was quite certain of this when she listened to the story.

"But why didn't your uncle help you?" Marie asked, as she became more and more impressed with the idea that the battle she had witnessed was to save the kingdom and crown of the Nutcracker. Had she not seen that all the other dolls were his subjects and was it not a fact that the prophecy of the court astronomer had been fulfilled and young Mr. Drosselmeier had become king of the dolls?

During the time that clever Marie was turning this over in her mind, she believed that the Nutcracker and his vassals must really come to life and begin to move. But this was not the case, everything in the cupboard remained quiet and motionless. Marie, however, unwilling to give up her idea, was convinced that this was due to the evil spell cast upon them by Mrs. Mouserinks and her seven-headed son. Out loud she said, "Even if you are not able to move or speak to me, dear Mr. Drosselmeier, I know that you understand how good my intentions are. You may count on my assistance, whenever you need it. At least I shall ask your uncle to help you with his skill, should it be necessary." The Nutcracker remained quiet, but to Marie it seemed as if a sigh which seemed to resound from the panes of glass, could be heard throughout the cupboard.

It was twilight when Marie's father and Judge Drosselmeier made their appearance. In a short time Luise had the tea table ready and the family gathered around it, each one having something amusing to tell. Marie had brought her little easy chair and seated herself at the side of Godfather Drosselmeier. Just when there was a moment of silence, Marie looked up at the judge with her large blue eyes and said:

"I am now convinced, dear Godfather, that my Nutcracker is your nephew, the young Mr. Drosselmeier from Nuremberg. He is a prince, or rather a king, as was foretold by your companion, the astronomer, but you know he is at open war with the son of Mrs. Mouserinks, the mean Mouse King. Why don't you help him?"

Marie now repeated the entire details of the battle as she had witnessed it, and was often interrupted by the loud laughter of her mother and Luise. Only Fritz and the judge remained serious.

"Where does the girl get such foolish notions?" asked her father.

"She has a lively imagination—it really is more of a dream, brought about by the fever from the wound in her arm," replied her mother.

"It isn't all true," cried Fritz, "for my red hussars are not such poltroons, or I would see to them."

Smiling, the judge took Marie on his lap and whispered, "You, dear Marie, have been favored above the rest of us. You are like Pirlipat, a born princess, for you reign over a bright kingdom. But you will suffer much, if you are going to defend the poor, misshapen Nutcracker, as the Mouse King is following him into every highway and byway. But not I—only you, you alone can save him, be steadfast and loyal."

THE VICTORY

Not long after this, Marie was awakened on a bright moonlight night by a peculiar noise, which seemed to come from the corner of the room. It sounded as though little stones were being unloaded, and with it a loud cracking and squeaking was heard.

"Oh! The mice, the mice are here again," cried Marie and wanted to call her mother, but she couldn't utter a sound, nor move a limb. She saw the Mouse King push himself through a hole in the floor and run about the room with his seven pairs of sparkling eyes and his seven crowns.

With one leap he jumped on the table that stood beside Marie's bed and said, "Hi-hi-hi! Give me your sugar plums, your marzipan, little girl—or else I will bite your Nutcracker—your Nutcracker." So hissed the Mouse King, showing his teeth; then he jumped down and ran into the hole.

Marie was so frightened at the ugly apparition, that she was quite pale the next morning and was so excited that she could hardly talk. Over and over again, she thought she would tell her mother or Luise, or at least Fritz, what had happened to her, but she always decided, "They will not believe me and will only laugh at me." It was very clear to her, however, that if she wished to save the Nutcracker she would have to sacrifice her sugar plums and marzipan. All she had of these she therefore laid on the ledge of the cupboard.

In the morning her mother called her and said, "I cannot understand how it is we have mice in our living room now. Just see, Marie, they have eaten all your candy." It was really so—all the candy was gone except a few pieces for which the greedy Mouse King evidently did not care. They were nibbled at and had to be thrown away. Marie did not grieve about this, however, as she was overjoyed at believing she had saved her Nutcracker.

But lo and behold! The following night close to her ear there was the same squeaking and hissing. Oh! The Mouse King was there again, and his eyes sparkled more meanly than the night before, as he hissed through his teeth, "You will have to give me your sugar cookies and your dolls, or I will bite the Nutcracker," and then the mean Mouse King ran away again. Marie was very sad.

The next morning she went to the cupboard and looked at all her pretty candy dolls, for here was a shepherd with his sheep, a letter carrier with letters in his hand, and four pretty couples, nicely dressed young men with especially beautiful girls, were swinging in a Russian dance. Just back of a few dancers were Joan of Arc and a companion. For these Marie cared little, but in the corner was a red-cheeked candy baby, her favorite—and then she burst into tears.

"Oh," she called, turning to the Nutcracker, "dear Mr. Drosselmeier, I will do anything to save you, but it surely is not easy." Nutcracker seemed so grieved when she looked at him that she at once decided to sacrifice all her dolls and again placed them on the ledge of the cupboard. She kissed the shepherd and his lambs, and at last also brought out her favorite, the little red-cheeked baby, which she placed in the back row, putting Joan of Arc and her companion in the front row.

"Why this is quite dreadful," cried Marie's mother the next morning. "There must be a large, mean mouse in the cupboard, for all of Marie's pretty candy dolls have been nibbled and partly eaten." Marie could hardly keep from crying, but when she remembered that it was to save the Nutcracker, she smiled again. In the evening Mrs. Stahlbaum was telling her husband and the judge about the havoc that a large mouse was causing in the cupboard. They all seemed to think that there should be some way to get rid of it.

"I know how," said Fritz, "the baker next door has a fine tom cat. I will get him up here and he will soon put an end to such a mouse, even if she is Mrs. Mouserinks, or her son, the Mouse King."

"Yes," replied his father, "and he will jump on every chair and table, and break glasses and cups and cause much damage."

"Oh, I don't think so—the baker's cat is a very clever fellow, and I only wish I could balance on the edge of the roof the way he does."

"No cat at night time, please," called Luise, who had an aversion for them. "Of course, we can set up a trap—haven't we one in the house?"

"Godfather Drosselmeier can make one for us," called Fritz, "he is the inventor of them."

Everybody laughed at this, and upon the assurance of Mrs. Stahlbaum that there was no mousetrap in the house, the judge at once had one brought from his home.

Fritz and Marie now had lively recollections of their godfather's "Fairy Tale of the Hard Nut" and when the cook fried the bacon, Marie said to Dora, "Madam Queen, you had better be on your guard against Mrs. Mouserinks and her family."

Fritz, however, drew his sword and said, "I would show them if they came near." But everything above and below the hearth remained quiet. When the judge fastened the bacon in the trap, and very cautiously placed the trap in the cupboard, Fritz called, "You had better be very careful, Godfather Watchmaker, that the Mouse King will not play some tricks on you."

The next night Marie was much more excited. Something icy cold was tapping on her arm and there was something rough against her cheek which squeaked and hissed in her ear. It was the mean Mouse King sitting on her shoulder and with his teeth grinding and grating, he hissed into her ear. She was unable to move for fright.

Hush, hush, I'll not go in the house—give all you have, your picture books, your dresses, or you will have no peace—for you must know Nutcracker will be bitten—hi, hi, squeak, squeak."

Now Marie was filled with sorrow and distress. She looked pale and anxious the next morning. Her mother, thinking Marie was grieving about her dolls and also afraid of the mouse, said, "Do not worry, dear child, we will get rid of the ugly mouse. If the trap does not catch this mouse, we will take Fritz's advice and get the baker's tom cat."

As soon as Marie found herself alone in the living room, she went at once to the cupboard and sobbing said, "Oh my dear Mr. Drosselmeier, what can I, poor, unhappy girl do for you? Even if I give my picture books and my very pretty dress which Santa brought me, for the Mouse King to gnaw on, will he not at last want me and bite me? What shall I do now, what shall I do?"

When Marie was thus lamenting, she noticed that a spot of blood had remained on the neck of the Nutcracker since that eventful night. She took him carefully from the shelf and began to rub the spot with her handkerchief. But she could hardly believe her senses, for when she was rubbing, she felt the Nutcracker coming to life in her hand. Quickly she returned him to the shelf and then his little mouth quivered, and he whispered, "My dear Marie, loyal friend, how much I owe to you—no, no picture book nor Christmas dress shall you sacrifice for me—just produce a sword—a sword, and leave the rest to me." Here he became speechless, and his sad, expressive eyes again were lifeless.

Marie was no longer afraid. In fact, she was overjoyed for now she knew a remedy that would help the Nutcracker without any more painful sacrifices on her part. But where should she get a sword for the little fellow? Marie decided to confide in Fritz; and as their parents were away, and they were alone in the living room, she again told him the whole story and asked his advice about saving the Nutcracker.

"As far as the sword is concerned, I can help the Nutcracker, for I retired an old colonel with pension a few days ago, and he will have no more use for his beautiful sharp sword." Fritz at once brought forth the colonel from the corner of the third shelf, where he was apparently enjoying his pension, relieved him of his silver sword and fastened it on the Nutcracker.

Being much afraid, Marie could not go to sleep the following night. About midnight she thought she heard queer noises in the living room. All at once she heard a squeak. "The Mouse King, the Mouse King," called Marie and sprang, badly scared, out of the bed.

Everything was quiet, but soon she heard a knocking on the door and a low voice whispered, "Dear Miss Stahlbaum, you can safely open the door, I have good news."

Marie recognized the voice of young Mr. Drosselmeier, slipped into her dress and quickly opened the door. There stood the Nutcracker, with the bloody sword in his right hand and in his left a candle.

As soon as he saw Marie, he knelt on one knee and said, "You, dear lady, are the one who gave me the courage of a knight, and the strength of my arms to subdue this insolent fellow. Conquered, the treacherous Mouse King is now destroyed. Will you, dear lady, accept from the hand of your devoted knight, yours until death, the proof of victory?" With this the Nutcracker slipped from his arm the seven golden crowns of the Mouse King and handed them to Marie, who was delighted with the gift.

Nutcracker then stood up and continued, "Oh, Miss Stahlbaum, what wonderful things I could show you at this moment when I have subdued my enemy, if you would favor me and follow me a few steps. Oh, favor me and come, dear lady."

The Kingdom of the Dolls

Marie was well aware that she was entitled to Nutcracker's gratitude and was convinced that he would keep his word and show her many wonderful things. "I will go, Mr. Drosselmeier, but it must not be far nor take too long, as I have not had my Night's sleep. I will choose, therefore," replied Nutcracker, "the nearest way, even if a little more difficult."

He walked ahead and Marie followed him, until he stood before the large heavy wardrobe in the hall. Marie was astonished to see that the doors of this cupboard, which were usually securely locked, stood open, and she could distinctly see her father's traveling fox furs hanging in front. Nutcracker climbed very skillfully up on the ledge and onto the moulding, in order to reach the large tassel which was fastened to a heavy cord on the back of the fur coat. When Nutcracker gave a jerk on the tassel, a dainty flight of cedar wood steps came down through the sleeve.

"Will you be good enough to go up?" called Nutcracker. Marie did as she was asked but had hardly gone through the sleeve and looked out at the collar when a blinding light met her view and she found herself in the center of a meadow, heavy with fragrance, from which millions of sparks were shining forth like glittering diamonds.

"We are now in the candy meadow," said Nutcracker, "but we shall soon pass out through that gateway." Now Marie became aware of a beautiful gate arising a few steps from them in the meadow. It seemed to be built of white, brown, and pink speckled marble, but when she came nearer, she saw that the entire mass was baked out of sugar, almonds, and raisins.

"For this reason," Nutcracker explained, "it was known as the Almond-Raisin Gate." On a protruding gallery of this gate, seemingly of barley sugar, six little monkeys in red waistcoats were producing beautiful music. Soon Marie was surrounded by the most delicious fragrance, which came from a nearby forest. In the dark foliage there was so much that was sparkling and glistening that one could see quite distinctly gold and silver fruit hanging on brightly colored stems. The trunks and branches were adorned with ribbons and flowers, like a bridal couple and their merry guests. And when the orange perfume floated like waves, the branches and leaves murmured, the tinsel crackled and rustled, like joyful music, to the accompaniment of which the sparkling lights were skipping and dancing.

"Oh! How beautiful it is here," cried Marie, she was so happy and delighted.

"We are in the Christmas Forest, dearest Fraulein," said Nutcracker.

"Oh! If only I could stay here a little while," said Marie, "it is so lovely." Nutcracker clapped his little hands and immediately appeared some shepherds and shepherdesses, hunters, and huntresses, who were so delicate and white that they seemed to be made of pure sugar. They brought forth a most lovely feudal chair of solid gold, laid a white, glossy cushion in it and very politely invited Marie to recline on it. Scarcely had she done so when the shepherds and shepherdesses danced a graceful ballet for which the hunters whistled. Then they all disappeared in the shrubbery.

"You will pardon," said Nutcracker, "that the dance was such a failure, but these people are all tight-rope walkers and can only do the same thing over and over again. There is also a reason for the music being so weak—the pastry hangs just above their heads in the Christmas trees, but too high to reach. Shall we not walk on?"

"Oh! How beautiful and charming it is here, and it certainly delights me," said Marie getting up and following Nutcracker, who had gone ahead.

They walked along a murmuring brook from which a delicious fragrance seemed to come, filling the entire forest. "It is the Orange Brook," said Nutcracker when questioned, "but except for its fragrance it does not compare with Lemonade River, which like it, flows into Almond-Milk Lake." In fact, Marie soon heard a louder splashing and rippling and saw the broad Lemonade River proudly threading its course in cream-colored waves through the green, glowing shrubbery.

A refreshing cool air, which strengthened chest and heart, arose from this water. Not far away, a slow, dark, yellow stream was quietly wending its fragrant way. On its shores pretty little children were catching plump fish, which they ate at once. In the distance on this river, Marie could see an imposing village. Houses, churches, barns were all dark brown, covered with golden roofs, and many walls were so colorfully decorated that it looked as if colored candies had been used in their construction.

"That is Sugar Cookie Village," said Nutcracker, "which lies on Honey River. The people living there are very handsome, but they are usually cross, for they suffer from toothache, and for that reason we will not stop there at present."

Just then Marie noticed a little city with gayly colored, transparent houses, which looked very attractive. Nutcracker went toward it and Marie heard an hilarious noise and saw thousands of neat little people unpacking high, loaded wagons in the market place. The cargo looked like bright colored papers and slabs of chocolate.

"We are in Bonbonville," said Nutcracker, "and a cargo has just arrived from Paperland and from the Chocolate King. The poor Bonbon houses were in great danger lately as they were attacked by an army of gnats and that is the reason, they are now covering their houses with the gifts from Paperland, and building trenches, supported by slabs from the Chocolate King. But, dear Fraulein Stahlbaum, we must not loiter in these villages, but visit the capital of this country."

Nutcracker hurried forward and Marie, full of curiosity, followed. In a few moments the air was filled with the fragrance of roses, and everything was tinged with a rosy hue. This, Marie noticed, was the reflection from a crimson lake, the waves of which were flowing along in silvery pink, while their splashing and murmuring produced beautiful tunes. On this shimmering water, silver-white swans with gold neckbands were swimming, and they joined in the melody, singing the most tuneful songs; while fishes like diamonds could be seen leaping up and down in this crimson water, as if taking part in the merriest dance.

"Oh!" cried Marie, "that is the lake that Godfather Drosselmeier was going to make for me, and I am the little girl who is going to feed the swans."

Nutcracker smiled ironically, which Marie had never seen him do before and replied, "Your Godfather could never produce anything like this."

THE CANDY CAPITAL

Nutcracker again clapped his little hands, and at once the crimson lake murmured louder and the waves splashed higher, and in the distance, Marie saw a gayly colored, opalescent shell wagon sparkling with all sorts of gems and drawn by two dolphins with golden scales. Twelve little boys, with caps and aprons woven from the feathers of hummingbirds leaped to the shore and carried first Marie and then the Nutcracker over the waves into the wagon, which then glided over the lake.

Oh how glorious it was to ride in this shell wagon, surrounded by rose perfume and rosy waves. The two gold-scaled dolphins lifted their nostrils and gushed forth high into the air crystal jets of water and as these fell in rainbow colors, one could hear two silver-toned voices saying, "Who swims on the lake so airy? The fairy, the fairy, bim, bim—little fishes swim, swim—Swans, move and sing, and the fairies bring, rosy waves dash, clash, flash—ever on."

The twelve pages who had jumped on the back of the shell wagon seemed to resent the song of the water, for they shook their parasols so violently that the date leaves from which they were made crackled and spluttered. With that they stamped their feet and sang, "Click-clack, click-clack, forward and back—dancers cannot be slack; fishes and swans bestir yourself, drone shell wagon, drone—click-clack, forward and back."

"These dancers are very merry people," said Nutcracker, "but if they keep on they will drive the whole lake into rebellion." It was true, for soon one could hear a deafening noise of wonderful voices coming from the air and water. Marie was not disturbed, however, as she saw only charming girls' faces smiling at her from the waves.

"Oh!" she cried, clapping her hands. "Oh! Look, dear Mr. Drosselmeier; there is Princess Pirlipat smiling at me. Oh look, look!"

Nutcracker, however, sighed rather sadly and said, "That is not Princess Pirlipat, that is yourself, always your own face, that smiles from each rosy wave."

In that moment the twelve pages picked her up and carried her to the shore. She found herself in a green thicket, which seemed even more wonderful than the Christmas Forest, for everything sparkled and glistened. Especially marvelous were the rare fruits of the strangest color and fragrance, hanging on the trees.

"We are in the Confetti Grove," said Nutcracker, "and over there is the capital."

What did Marie see there? Not only were the walls and towers gayly colored, but the shape of the buildings was different from anything she had seen on earth. Instead of roofs, these houses had dainty braided crowns and the towers were decorated with the most delicate foliage she had ever seen. As she passed through the gateway, which looked as if it were built of macaroons and candied fruit, silver soldiers stood at "Attention" and one little man in a brocaded dressing-gown threw his arms around Nutcracker's neck with the words, "Welcome, dear Prince, welcome to Confectionville."

Marie was rather astonished to have the Nutcracker addressed as "Prince" by such a distinguished gentleman. But in a moment, she heard so many voices cheering and laughing, so much music and singing, that she could think of nothing else and asked Nutcracker to explain the meaning of all this.

Nutcracker replied, "This is nothing unusual. This is a well-populated, merry city and this happens every day. Come this way, please."

They had gone but a few steps when they came to the large marketplace, which presented the most gorgeous view. The buildings around it were made of fancy pastry, all having many galleries. In the center stood a high, candied cake like an obelisk. This was the tree cake, and around it four artificial fountains sent forth lemonade and other sweet drinks. In the basin were all kinds of ice creams, and ices to which one wanted to help oneself.

But prettier than all this were the little people, who were there by the thousands moving in great throngs, shouting, laughing, and joking. In short, they produced the uproar Marie had heard from a distance. Here were handsomely dressed ladies and gentlemen, Armenians, Greeks, and Tyroleans, officers and soldiers, ministers, shepherds, and clowns, in fact, people of every kind that are found in the world.

On one corner the tumult became louder as the people made way for the great mogul who was being carried by in a palanquin, accompanied by ninety-three dignitaries of the realm and seven hundred slaves. It so happened, however, that on the other corner, the fisherman's guild of five hundred were having their procession. The Turkish mogul also just had decided to ride over the market square with three thousand soldiers. Added to this a large troop from the opera came by, who with a full band were triumphantly singing, "Up, thank the mighty sun," making straight for the cake. There certainly was a pushing, a crowding, and a noisy carrying on.

Soon one heard great cries of distress, for in the crowding a fisherman had knocked off the head of an Indian priest, and the grand mogul was nearly run over by a clown. The noise grew louder and louder, and the crowd was beginning to be so boisterous that many were fighting, when the gentleman in the brocaded dressing gown, who had greeted the Nutcracker as prince at the gate, climbed up the tree cake.

After a very clear-toned bell had rung three times, he called three times very loudly, "Pastry cook, pastry cook, pastry cook." At once the noise ceased and after each procession was again in order, the soiled grand mogul had been cleaned up and the Indian priest's head had been replaced, the noise went on as before.

"Why does he call a pastry cook, Mr. Drosselmeier?" asked Marie.

"Oh! Fraulein," answered Nutcracker, "pastry and confectionery have a great power here, as it is believed that with them one can make anything one wants of any person. The little merry people are so afraid of this power that the mere mention of the word will quiet the greatest tumult, which the mayor has just proven to you. No one then thinks of anything earthly, of the blow in his side, or of a black eye, but turns his thoughts inward and says, 'What is man and what can be made of him?'"

Marie now could not refrain from a loud exclamation of wonder for she stood before a palace with one hundred towers all lighted with crimson glowing lights. Here and there on the walls were large bouquets of violets, narcissus, tulips, and stocks, the rich colors of which enhanced the white of the building with their pink glow. The large dome of the center building, as well as the pyramid-shaped towers, was strewn with thousands of sparkling gold and silver stars.

"Now we are before the Marzipan Castle," said Nutcracker.

Marie was speechless before this enchanted palace, but she noticed that the roof of one of the large towers was entirely missing and that little men standing on a scaffold of cinnamon sticks were trying to restore it.

Before Marie could ask for an explanation, the Nutcracker continued, "A short time ago this palace was threatened with a wicked devastation, if not with entire destruction. The Giant Sweet Tooth came this way, and quickly bit into the roof of yonder tower and was nibbling on the dome when the citizens of this city bought him off by giving him as a tribute an entire quarter of the city as well as a part of the grove. This satisfied his appetite, and he went on."

At this moment one could hear soft, low music, the doors of the palace were opened, and twelve pages came out carrying torches of stems of cloves in their little hands. Their heads consisted of one pearl, the body of rubies and emeralds, and they walked on feet made of pure gold. They were followed by four ladies about the size of Marie's new doll, but so exquisitely dressed that Marie at once knew they must be princesses.

They embraced Nutcracker most affectionately and cried in a sad voice, "Oh, my prince, my dear prince. Oh, my brother!"

Nutcracker seemed elated but sad, for he wiped the tears from his eyes, took hold of Marie's hand and spoke in a formal manner, "This is Fraulein Marie Stahlbaum, who saved my life, the daughter of a very honorable physician. If she had not thrown her slipper at the right time and procured for me the sword of the retired colonel, I would by this time be in my grave bitten to pieces by that cursed Mouse King." Turning to Marie they cried, "Oh! Are you like Pirlipat, although she is a born princess, in beauty, goodness, and virtue?"

"No, no," cried Marie. All the ladies cried, "Yes, yes," and embraced Marie, sobbing, "Oh, noble savior of our beloved princely brother."

Now the ladies escorted Marie and Nutcracker into the interior of the palace, into a room the walls of which were made of different-colored crystals. But Marie liked best of all the dear little chairs, tables, bureaus, and other furniture standing all around which were made of mahogany and teak wood decorated with gold flowers. The princess urged Marie and Nutcracker to be seated and said they would at once prepare a meal.

They then brought out a quantity of little dishes of all kinds of the finest Japanese porcelain, spoons, knives and forks, a grater, casseroles, and other kitchen utensils of gold and silver. They brought the most delicious fruits and pastry, such as Marie had never seen, and with their dainty white hands prepared the fruit, grated the almonds, pounded the spices—in short, did what was necessary, and Marie could see at once how well they knew how to prepare a delicious meal. In fact, if the truth were known, she was wishing that she too might help. The most beautiful of Nutcracker's sisters, as if reading her thoughts, handed her a gold mortar with the words, "Oh dear friend, beloved deliverer of my brother, pound a little of this loaf sugar."

While Marie was merrily pounding in the mortar, sounding as it did, like a pretty tune, Nutcracker began to relate how in the fierce battle between him and the army of the Mouse King, he was defeated, owing to the cowardice of his own troops, and how the ugly Mouse King was then about to devour him, when Marie came to his rescue by offering a number of her subjects as tribute. It seemed to Marie, while listening to this story, that Nutcracker's words, yes, even her pounding, were fading away into the distance, and she saw silver gauze, like thin fog clouds, rising in the air, in which the princesses, pages, Nutcracker, yes, even she herself were floating—she could hear a queer singing, buzzing, and chirping which was growing less and less, and then as if in a cloud she was going higher—higher and higher—higher and higher.

CONCLUSION

Purr-Puff, it went—Marie fell down from this immense height. That was an awful shock.

She opened her eyes at once—there she lay in her bed, it was daytime and her mother was standing by her and said, "How can anyone sleep so late, it is long past breakfast time!"

"Oh Mother, dear Mother," stuttered Marie and looked around somewhat dazed, "where have I been, where did young Mr. Drosselmeier take me last night and what wonderful things did I see?"

Then she began to tell her story. Her mother looked at her most astonished. When Marie finished her mother said, "You have had a long and very beautiful dream, my child, but now you must forget it." Marie insisted, however, that she had not been dreaming, but that she had seen it all. Then her mother led her to the cupboard, took the Nutcracker from the third shelf and said, "How can you insist that this Nuremberg wooden doll could come to life?"

"But, dear Mother," replied Marie, "I know full well that the Nutcracker is young Mr. Drosselmeier of Nuremberg and a nephew of our godfather." At this Marie's father and mother both burst into hearty peals of laughter.

"Oh!" said Marie, almost crying, "now you are laughing at my Nutcracker, dear father, and you should have heard how well he spoke of you, for when we arrived at the Marzipan Palace he introduced me to his sisters, the princesses, and said my father was a most estimable physician."

At this they laughed louder than ever, even Luise and Fritz joining in. Then Marie ran into the other room and brought from her little chest the seven crowns of the Mouse King and, handing them to her mother, said, "See, dear Mother, those are the seven crowns which young Mr. Drosselmeier gave me last night, as a proof of his victory."

Much astonished, they all looked at the little crowns, which were made up of an unknown, but very bright, metal. The work was so skillful that it seemed almost impossible that human hands could have accomplished it. The Doctor, much in earnest, began to ask Marie where she had obtained these crowns, but she insisted she had already told them. And when her father became impatient and said she was not truthful, she burst into tears and said, "There is nothing else for me to tell you."

At that moment the door opened, and the judge entered. "Why, what has happened here, why is my good child crying and sobbing?" he asked. Marie's father told him the story and showed him the crowns.

When the judge looked at these, he laughed and exclaimed, "Nonsense, nonsense, those are the little crowns that years ago I used to wear on my watch chain, and which I gave to Marie on her second birthday. Don't you remember that?"

But no one seemed to have any recollection of this, and when Marie saw that they all were friendly again, she ran over to the judge and said:

"You know everything, Godfather, and you also know that my Nutcracker is your nephew from Nuremberg, and that he gave me the little crowns." At this they all became serious and commanded Marie to stop imagining anything more or she would be punished.

Now, of course, Marie could not speak any more of her strange adventure, but the pictures of the fairy kingdom played around her in billowy waves of sweetest ripples and in charming, lovely sounds. She thought about it again and again, so much so that she could sit quietly and not play, and they at last called her a dreamer.

Yes, in the merry Christmas time children dream wonderful things. And beautiful dreams are also fairy tales, as is this one of the Nutcracker and the Mouse King.

ABOUT THE AUTHOR

E. T. A. HOFFMAN (1776–1822) was a German author at the forefront of the Romantic movement in the early nineteenth century. A composer, too, he took the middle name Amadeus out of admiration for Mozart. It is only fitting that two of Hoffman's stories were later turned into full-length ballets with beautiful music—*Coppélia* and *The Nutcracker*.

A Bit of History

In the tale of "The Nutcracker and the Mouse King," meaning is created through the characters' names just as much as through its pages. The surname of Marie—Stahlbaum—means steel tree in German, a testament to the formality and restrictive nature of Marie's family. The exception to the rule is her godfather Drosselmeier, whose name roughly means someone who stirs up trouble and contrasts starkly with the larger Stahlbaum family. The nomenclature of "The Nutcracker and the Mouse King" is directly reflective of the plot, a bit of knowledge that enhances the story and reminds us of the importance of expanding our horizons to appreciate other cultures and languages.

The story was first published in Germany in 1816 as part of the *Kinder-Märchen* collection and was first translated into English in 1853. Alexandre Dumas' adaptation of the short story served as the basis for Pyotr Tchaikovsky's balletic interpretation, simply called *The Nutcracker*.

BABOUSCKA

By Bailey and Lewis

ORIGINALLY FROM *FOR THE CHILDREN'S HOUR* STORY COLLECTION

It was the night the dear Christ Child came to Bethlehem. In a country far away from Him, an old, old woman named Babouscka sat in her snug little house by her warm fire. The wind was drifting the snow outside and howling down the chimney, but it only made Babouscka's fire burn more brightly.

"How glad I am that I may stay indoors!" said Babouscka, holding her hands out to the bright blaze. But suddenly she heard a loud rap at her door. She opened it and her candle shone on three old men standing outside in the snow. Their beards were as white as the snow, and so long that they reached the ground. Their eyes shone kindly in the light of Babouscka's candle, and their arms were full of precious things—boxes of jewels, and sweet-smelling oils, and ointments.

"We have traveled far, Babouscka," said they, "and we stop to tell you of the Baby Prince born this night in Bethlehem. He comes to rule the world and teach all men to be loving and true. We carry Him gifts. Come with us, Babouscka!"

But Babouscka looked at the driving snow, and then inside at her cozy room and the crackling fire. "It is too late for me to go with you, good sirs," she said, "the weather is too cold." She went inside again and shut the door, and the old men journeyed on to Bethlehem without her. But as Babouscka sat by her fire, rocking, she began to think about the little Christ Child, for she loved all babies.

"Tomorrow I will go to find Him," she said, "tomorrow, when it is light, and I will carry Him some toys."

So when it was morning Babouscka put on her long cloak, and took her staff, and filled a basket with the pretty things a baby would like—gold balls, and wooden toys, and strings of silver cobwebs—and she set out to find the Christ Child.

But, oh! Babouscka had forgotten to ask the three old men the road to Bethlehem, and they had traveled so far through the night that she could not overtake them. Up and down the roads she hurried, through woods and fields and towns, saying to whomsoever she met: "I go to find the Christ Child. Where does he lie? I bring some pretty toys for His sake."

But no one could tell her the way to go, and they all said: "Farther on, Babouscka, farther on." So she traveled on, and on, and on for years and years—but she never found the little Christ Child.

They say that old Babouscka is traveling still, looking for Him. When it comes Christmas Eve, and the children are lying fast asleep, Babouscka comes softly through the snowy fields and towns, wrapped in her long cloak and carrying her basket on her arm. With her staff she raps gently at the doors and goes inside and holds her candle close to the little children's faces.

"Is He here?" she asks. "Is the little Christ Child here?" And then she turns sorrowfully away again, crying: "Farther on, farther on." But before she leaves, she takes a toy from her basket and lays it beside the pillow for a Christmas gift. "For His sake," she says softly, and then hurries on through the years and forever in search of the little Christ Child.

About the Author

CAROLYN S. BAILEY (1875–1961) started her writing journey as a contributor to magazines like *Ladies' Home Journal.* The American author eventually transitioned into a children's author with the goal of telling engaging yet teachable stories for kids. She won the Newbery Medal for her book *Miss Hickory* in 1947.

A Bit of History

Though this version of the story was created by Carolyn S. Bailey, "Babouscka" is an old Russian legend which cannot be traced back to one single author. The word *babouscka* has two meanings in the language: a grandmother or an elderly woman, and a head scarf. Both encapsulate the mythic image of the woman who, in this telling, spends an eternity waiting to find the Christ Child. Though variations of the story have been published in anthologies since the late 1800s, the true source of it is unknown.

Several songs and a music group revolving around the Legend of Babouscka have also emerged since the 1970s, a testament to the original oral form of the story. "Babouscka" serves as a reminder of the power of oral histories and how they can be just as important and enduring as their written form.

Up On The Housetop

Benjamin Hanby

Jolly Old Saint Nicholas

BITS

By Helen G. Ricks

· Originally from *The Crisis*, Volume 13, No. 2

The feathery snowflakes came hurrying down simply because it was the day before Christmas and not because there was any intention on their part to remain. It was late afternoon and the holiday bustle had only partially subsided.

Pushing through the crowds at the railway station, a young girl emerged, muffled up to the ears in furs, with a girlish face wreathed up to the eyes in smiles. It was very evident with her that Christmas was coming. At the gate entrance she inquired about her train. The *train was gone!* To stand there stupidly gazing at the official who certainly was not responsible helped matters not at all. Of course, it meant a "wire" and a wait until next morning. To a girl who was bent on meeting a bunch of college friends at a house party Christmas morning, the laconic information concerning the means of her transportation came not joyously. The tears which filled her brown eyes were definitely feminine. And then a little smile slipped out from somewhere and she proceeded to the Western Union office.

She was pushing through the door leading out to the busy street when a little brown hand caught at her skirt.

"*Evenin' Herald*, Lady?"

The girl looked down.

"Why, little fellow, you're crying. I can't let you take my pet indulgence away from me like that. Tell me about things, dear." And she brushed a perfectly good little tear out of the corner of her eye—the one that had refused to be chased when the smile came.

"It's—it's that I've just got to sell out tonight. It's—it's oranges for Bits."

By this time the ragged little coat-sleeve was serving wonderfully as a handkerchief.

"Come, come, little lad, stand over here out of the crowd. Somehow I don't understand. Who is Bits?"

"Why, he's all I've got—that's all."

"Oh, I see! Can't you tell me more about him and your own little self? Maybe I can buy you out?"

The childish face stared up into the girl's with an incredulity that was not at all concealed.

"Mean it, or jes' kiddin'?"

"Yes, dear, I *do* mean it. Tell me."

"It ain't so awful much to tell you 'bout where we live, 'cause we ain't roomin' in any manshun. Bits an' Spatch an' me all sleeps on a cot in Mis' Barney's basement, an' we gets our feed from Greeley's grocery when we *gets* it. Spatch is jes' beany 'bout weenies—swellest little poor dog you ever seen. We ain't got no folks but jes' ourselves, an' Spatch. Somehow, though, Bits hits it off with the papers—he's onto *his* job all right. I'm littler than him an' folks lots of time passes me up. We ain't never had *heaps*, but we has allus been happy, 'cause Bits says it's the only way to top off things. He's sick, though, now—he jes' all to oncet took down an' they bustled him off to the hospital. He looked right spruce an' cleaned up in that white bed when I went to see him, but say, he was *some* sick. They told me I could come back tonight, an' I wanted *awful* hard to take him oranges 'cause tomorrer's Christmas. But you see, I'm down to six cents, less'n I sell out. Guess I wasn't a game thoroughbred, like when you saw me crying—bet you Bits wouldn't a done it! My name's Rodney, but folks as knows me calls me Pep, 'cause some days I hits it off right spunky—'specially when they're hot on—on Spatch's trail—he's one-eyed."

With the ingeniousness of the small boy, he related the history of himself, Bits and Spatch. And the girl understood.

"Rodney, I'm going to buy you out and we'll dispose of these *Heralds* someway. You lead the way because we must get these oranges to Bits. May I go with you, please, to see your brother?"

"Well, I should jes' bet you can! It ain't so far, but I spect' as how you'll better take the car. I'm only got six cents, but I'll boost you up an' pop the conductor a half-dime an' beat it faster than the car an' be *waitin'* for you."

"Thank you, dear, for wishing for me to ride, but oh, I'd love to walk with you if I may."

"Say, you are some great—know it?"

And the look of gallant appreciation overspread the boy's face.

"Maybe if you're this good for walkin'—maybe you wouldn't mind cuttin' over two blocks with me. I promised Spatch that *he* could go tonight."

"Certainly! Are you cold, dear?"

"Should say not—too excited!"

They were reaching the quarter of the city very unfamiliar to the girl. Faithfully she followed the little figure striding along manfully with a bundle of *Evenin' Heralds* tucked under one arm.

"'Lo, kids!"

They had passed a bunch of little street children.

"That's my bunch. They was some starin'—huh? Wonderin' bout you, I guess."

Finally, they had reached a tenement house.

"Can't ast you in, but I'll be right down soon as I untie him. An'—an' shall I leave these papers? She could use them for kindlin'."

"Oh, yes, by all means! I'll wait for you."

In an incredibly short space of time a boy with a dog was retracing his steps down the street in company with the girl.

"Ain't he a dog fer you? Spatch is the cut'off for 'Dispatch'—one of the old papers. We're *pardners!*"

His new friend smiled understandingly.

At the fruit stand they purchased the oranges.

"Say! But you're *some* lady. I'll bet Bits will like you heaps. What made you good to me today?"

"Why, my dear! I just love all the little boys and girls of my race. I just wanted to help you if I could, just a little bit."

They had now reached the hospital. The girl, the small boy, and the dog entered the building. It so happened that the lady visitor was not a stranger to the hospital force, consequently Spatch was graciously accorded a permit.

"How is the little lad, nurse?"

"The crisis came four nights ago—he will recover. He's been waiting for his little brother—go right in."

The white hospital cot was near the window and a shaft of light fell across the face, which instantly became illumined with a smile when Spatch and Pep uttered their effusive greetings.

"Well, if here ain't the little kid and Pardner! How's business? Sleep cold last night, Pep?"

"Should say not! So warm, almost had to hist the window!"

The tail of Spatch wagged perilously near the sack of oranges purposely concealed at the foot of the bed. Bits smiled, and then his eyes fell on the girl standing a little away from the bed. He turned towards Pep, and in a voice a trifle weak and very much puzzled, exclaimed: "Pep, who's the swell skirt? She with you?"

"She's some lady!" A smile followed his words, absolutely appreciative. "She bought me out an' then come clear here jes' to see you. Can't you shake? She's a—a friend of *mine*."

In the course of a few minutes *she* was irrevocably taken into the partnership with Bits, Pep, and Spatch. After the neighborhood news had been imparted and all the preliminaries completed, the oranges were presented. The smile from Bits more than paid their real value.

All too soon the nurse came to announce the close of visiting hours.

"Pep, old feller, cover up good tonight. Give Pardner a weenie and please take three of these oranges for yourself—tomorrer's Christmas. Stick it out! I'll be back to the old job soon. They're bully to me here."

The girl bent over the little sick-a-bed laddie.

"Bits, is there a single Christmas wish of yours that I could fulfill, dear? Please let me try."

"Mighty nice of you. I think you've done a heap now. But there is—is something. It's the little kid there. I've heard about juvenile officers an' their doin's. Mebbe *somebody* could get a home for him. He's a smart little chap, Miss, an' deserves a chance. When I get well, I'd work to help for his keep. Could you get him in?"

"Yes, dear, I've been thinking of Rodney all the way over here. Fortunately, I know the very people to secure him a home. And I have a friend who has charge of a settlement house, and I am going to take him there tonight, so he won't be lonesome. It's warm there, and they'll be good to him—they really would be happy to have him come. Plenty of boys there, and games, and a Christmas tree. I'll be there myself for a while. Now, have a good sleep and don't worry about him. Spatch is going, too. Good-bye."

As they turned to look back once more at the door, a smile from Bits was following them. Outside, Pep hesitated.

"Look here, I've *lied*—yes, I've told a ripper! I was freezin' cold last night—I give the blanket to my Pardner here."

"I understand, laddie. Tomorrow is Christmas. We're going downtown on this car and I'm going to fit you out in some real warm clothing for your Christmas present, Rodney. And then tonight you, and Spatch, and I, are going to the settlement house. There, other little colored children are having a Christmas tree, and games, and fun! And there isn't going to be any more paper selling for you, or Bits, but you're going to have a real home and a chance to go to school. I have friends who will help me. Are you willing, dear?"

Two little cold hands ecstatically clasped themselves over one of the girl's, and two little tears of joy made two little tracks on his childish brown face.

"I guess you're the 'Christmas Angel' I heard 'bout once. Gee! But you're touchin'!"

The happiness that reigned in his little heart that Christmas Eve is not to be described in words. Pep appreciated.

On Christmas morning a car stopped outside the settlement house and the girl bounded out to return leading a small boy, refreshed and happy and followed by a one-eyed canine disciple. All arrangements had been made and both boys were to be located in a private home with a fair chance. A young doctor, the very dearest friend of the girl's, had consented to look after her charges in her holiday absence. It was he who opened the door of the car as they approached.

"Good morning, little chap! Merry Christmas!"

"Ditto"—this last from Pep, and an exhilarating bark from Spatch.

"Rodney, this is Dr. Weston—our friend."

When they reached the ward, one bound and Pep was at the side of the bed.

"Know me, Bits? Some *looker*, ain't I? Had one spludge las' night—too big almost to talk about. She done it all. *She's an angel!* Now, hold your breath while I tell you the biggest ever! She's found a home for you, an' me, an' Spatch, an' we're going to school, an'—an' *she means it!*"

The "Christmas Angel" and the doctor came nearer the bed. Professionally he reached for the pulse and all the friendliness possible was in his greeting.

"Well, little friend, I'm in the partnership, too, and we're going to get you well in ten days!"

Bits smiled first at one and then at the others appreciatively.

"You two don't know how I thank you for myself an' the kid! I can't tell you. Just give us the chance—we'll prove up the claim!" Determination and gratitude were in his face.

"I'm glad if you're pleased, Bits. You are both going to be my little brothers, and Spatch here (at this opportune moment there was an appreciative tail-wag) is going to be our mascot. I must hurry now to catch the train, for I'm going away for three days. Dr. Weston is going to give Rodney a 'big day', and I think he has a surprise for Bits. Good-bye, dear!"

There was a kiss left on the warm forehead. A little hand shot out from the covering.

"You're the best Christmas I ever had! I—I just wish I could whisper to you, somethin'—"

The girl bent down. Two arms went around her neck, two words from a little heart filled with gratitude slipped out—

"Merry Christmas!"

ABOUT THE AUTHOR

Little is known about the real life of **HELEN G. RICKS**, who is only acknowledged in literary anthologies as an unfortunately "forgotten" African American author. The sole piece of writing credited to her name is the story "Bits," which first appeared in the 1916 Christmas edition of *The Crisis*.

A Bit of History

The official magazine of the NAACP, *The Crisis'* mission is to educate readers about the issues African Americans and other communities of color face through essays and short stories. Adhering to that mission in a more lighthearted manner, "Bits" showcases a young Black girl helping a poor little boy find a safe home to stay in on Christmas Eve. The immersive, heartwarming story still imparts important themes of class and race, and neither it nor its author will be forgotten.

LITTLE PICCOLA

By Frances Jenkins Olcott

Piccola lived in Italy, where the oranges grow, and where all the year the sun shines warm and bright. I suppose you think Piccola a very strange name for a little girl; but in her country it was not strange at all, and her mother thought it the sweetest name a little girl ever had.

Piccola had no kind father, no big brother or sister, and no sweet baby to play with and love. She and her mother lived all alone in an old stone house that looked on a dark, narrow street. They were very poor, and the mother was away from home almost every day, washing clothes and scrubbing floors, and working hard to earn money for her little girl and herself. So, you see Piccola was alone a great deal of the time; and if she had not been a very happy, contented little child, I hardly know what she would have done. She had no playthings except a heap of stones in the back yard that she used for building houses and a very old, very ragged doll that her mother had found in the street one day.

But there was a small round hole in the stone wall at the back of her yard, and her greatest pleasure was to look through that into her neighbor's garden. When she stood on a stone, and put her eyes close to the hole, she could see the green grass in the garden, and smell the sweet flowers, and even hear the water splashing into the fountain. She had never seen anyone walking in the garden, for it belonged to an old gentleman who did not care about grass and flowers.

One day in the autumn her mother told her that the old gentleman had gone away and had rented his house to a family of little American children, who had come with their sick mother to spend the winter in Italy. After this, Piccola was never lonely, for all day long the children ran and played and danced and sang in the garden. It was several weeks before they saw her at all, and I am not sure they ever would have done so but one day the kitten ran away, and in chasing her they came close to the wall and saw Piccola's black eyes looking through the hole in the stones. They were a little frightened at first and did not speak to her; but the next day she was there again, and Rose, the oldest girl, went up to the wall and talked to her a little while. When the children found that she had no one to play with and was very lonely, they talked to her every day, and often brought her fruits and candies, and passed them through the hole in the wall.

One day they even pushed the kitten through; but the hole was hardly large enough for her, and she mewed and scratched and was very much frightened. After that the little boy said he would ask his father if the hole might not be made larger, and then

Piccola could come in and play with them. The father had found out that Piccola's mother was a good woman, and that the little girl herself was sweet and kind, so that he was very glad to have some of the stones broken away and an opening made for Piccola to come in.

How excited she was, and how glad the children were when she first stepped into the garden! She wore her best dress, a long, bright-colored woolen skirt, and a white waist. Round her neck was a string of beads, and on her feet were little wooden shoes. It would seem very strange to us—would it not?—to wear wooden shoes; but Piccola and her mother had never worn anything else, and never had any money to buy stockings. Piccola almost always ran about barefooted, like the kittens and the chickens and the little ducks. What a good time they had that day, and how glad Piccola's mother was that her little girl could have such a pleasant, safe place to play in, while she was away at work!

By and by December came, and the little Americans began to talk about Christmas. One day, when Piccola's curly head and bright eyes came peeping through the hole in the wall, and they ran to her and helped her in; and as they did so, they all asked her at once what she thought she would have for a Christmas present. "A Christmas present!" said Piccola. "Why, what is that?"

All the children looked surprised at this, and Rose said, rather gravely, "Dear Piccola, don't you know what Christmas is?"

Oh, yes, Piccola knew it was the happy day when the baby Christ was born, and she had been to church on that day and heard the beautiful singing and had seen the picture of the Babe lying in the manger, with cattle and sheep sleeping round about. Oh, yes, she knew all that very well, but what was a Christmas present?

Then the children began to laugh and to answer her all together. There was such a clatter of tongues that she could hear only a few of the words now and then, such as "chimney," "Santa Claus," "stockings," "reindeer," "Christmas Eve," "candies and toys." Piccola put her hands over her ears and said, "Oh, I can't understand one word. You tell me, Rose." Then Rose told her all about jolly Santa Claus, with his red cheeks and white beard and fur coat, and about his reindeer and sleigh full of toys. "Every Christmas Eve," said Rose, "he comes down the chimney, and fills the stockings of all the good children; so, Piccola, you hang up your stocking, and who knows what a beautiful Christmas present you will find when morning comes!" Of course, Piccola thought this was a delightful plan, and was very pleased to hear about it. Then all the children told her of every Christmas Eve they could remember, and of the presents they had had; so that she went home thinking of nothing but dolls and hoops and balls and ribbons and marbles and wagons and kites.

She told her mother about Santa Claus, and her mother seemed to think that perhaps he did not know there was any little girl in that house, and very likely he would not come at all. But Piccola felt very sure Santa Claus would remember her, for her little friends had promised to send a letter up the chimney to remind him.

Christmas Eve came at last. Piccola's mother hurried home from her work; they had their little supper of soup and bread, and soon it was bedtime—time to get ready for Santa Claus. But oh! Piccola remembered then for the first time that the children had told her she must hang up her stocking, and she hadn't any, and neither had her mother.

How sad, how sad it was! Now Santa Claus would come, and perhaps be angry because he couldn't find any place to put the present.

The poor little girl stood by the fireplace, and the big tears began to run down her cheeks. Just then her mother called to her, "Hurry, Piccola; come to bed." What should she do? But she stopped crying and tried to think; and in a moment she remembered her wooden shoes and ran off to get one of them. She put it close to the chimney, and said to herself, "Surely Santa Claus will know what it's there for. He will know I haven't any stockings, so I gave him the shoe instead."

Then she went off happily to her bed and was asleep almost as soon as she had nestled close to her mother's side.

The sun had only just begun to shine, next morning, when Piccola awoke. With one jump she was out on the floor and running toward the chimney. The wooden shoe was lying where she had left it, but you could never, never guess what was in it.

Piccola had not meant to wake her mother, but this surprise was more than any little girl could bear and yet be quiet; so, she danced to the bed with the shoe in her hand, calling, "Mother, Mother! Look, look! See the present Santa Claus brought me!"

Her mother raised her head and looked into the shoe. "Why, Piccola," she said, "a little chimney swallow nestling in your shoe? What a good Santa Claus to bring you a bird!"

"Good Santa Claus, dear Santa Claus!" cried Piccola; and she kissed her mother and kissed the bird and kissed the shoe, and even threw kisses up the chimney, she was so happy.

When the birdling was taken out of the shoe, they found that he did not try to fly, only to hop about the room; and as they looked closer, they could see that one of his wings was hurt a little. But the mother bound it up carefully, so that it did not seem to pain him, and he was so gentle that he took a drink of water from a cup, and even ate crumbs and seeds out of Piccola's hands. She was a proud little girl when she took her Christmas present to show the children in the garden. They had had a great many gifts—dolls that could say "mamma," bright picture books, trains of cars, toy pianos; but not one of their playthings was alive, like Piccola's birdling. They were as pleased as she, and Rose hunted about the house until she found a large wicker cage that belonged to a blackbird she once had. She gave the cage to Piccola, and the swallow seemed to make himself quite at home in it at once and sat on the perch winking his bright eyes at the children. Rose had saved a bag of candies for Piccola, and when she went home at last, with the cage and her dear swallow safely inside it, I am sure there was not a happier little girl in the whole country of Italy.

About the Author

Frances Jenkins Olcott (1872–1963) developed a love for language from her parents, both translators who tutored her in French and German. In 1898, Olcott became the first head librarian of the Carnegie Library of Pittsburgh's children's department, where she worked until 1911. Afterwards, Olcott decided to become a children's writer herself, publishing and editing 24 volumes throughout her lifetime.

A Bit of History

The story of "Little Piccola" was inspired by a poem written by Celia Laighton Thaxter, an American writer and poet. The poem similarly follows Piccola as she discovers the Christmas gift of a bird, but lacks the same emphasis on cultural differences and adopting new traditions. The inclusion of this theme may be attributed to Olcott's upbringing, as she was exposed to many different cultures, values, and languages through her parents' experiences abroad. The change transformed the story from one about a memorable Christmas gift to one about exploring and accepting difference, a beautiful lesson for this holiday season.

"Little Piccola" was published by Olcott as part of a collection to help children practice their reading. The collection called *Good Stories for Great Holidays* was published in 1914.

THE FIR TREE

By Hans Christian Andersen

Included in the CHRISTMAS STORIES AND LEGENDS compilation

Far away in the forest, where the warm sun and the fresh air made a sweet resting place, grew a pretty little fir tree. The situation was all that could be desired; and yet it was not happy, it wished so much to be like its tall companions, the pines and firs which grew around it.

The sun shone, and the soft air fluttered its leaves, and the little peasant children passed by, prattling merrily; but the fir tree did not heed them.

Sometimes the children would bring a large basket of raspberries or strawberries, wreathed in straws, and seat themselves near the fir tree, and say, "Is it not a pretty little tree?" which made it feel even more unhappy than before.

And yet all this while the tree grew a notch or joint taller every year; for by the number of joints in the stem of a fir tree we can discover its age.

Still, as it grew, it complained: "Oh! how I wish I were as tall as the other trees; then I would spread out my branches on every side, and my crown would overlook the wide world around. I should have the birds building their nests on my boughs, and when the wind blew, I should bow with stately dignity, like my tall companions."

So discontented was the tree, that it took no pleasure in the warm sunshine, the birds, or the rosy clouds that floated over it morning and evening.

Sometimes in winter, when the snow lay white and glittering on the ground, there was a little hare that would come springing along and jump right over the little tree's head; then how mortified it would feel.

Two winters passed; and when the third arrived, the tree had grown so tall that the hare was obliged to run round it. Yet it remained unsatisfied, and would exclaim, "Oh! To grow, to grow; if I could but keep on growing tall and old! There is nothing else worth caring for in the world."

In the autumn the woodcutters came, as usual, and cut down several of the tallest trees; and the young fir, which was now grown to its full height, shuddered as the noble trees fell to the earth with a crash.

After the branches were lopped off, the trunks looked so slender and bare that they could scarcely be recognized. Then they were placed, one upon another, upon wagons, and drawn by horses out of the forest. "Where could they be going? What would become of them?" The young fir tree wished very much to know.

So, in the spring, when the swallows and the storks came, it asked, "Do you know where those trees were taken? Did you meet them?"

The swallows knew nothing; but the stork, after a little reflection, nodded his head and said, "Yes, I think I do. As I flew from Egypt, I saw several new ships, and they had fine masts that smelt like fir. These must have been the trees; and I assure you they were stately; they sailed right gloriously!"

"Oh, how I wish I were tall enough to go on the sea," said the fir tree. "Tell me, what is this sea, and what does it look like?"

"It would take too much time to explain, a great deal too much," said the stork, flying quickly away.

"Rejoice in thy youth," said the sunbeam; "rejoice in thy fresh growth, and in the young life that is in thee."

And the wind kissed the tree, and the dew watered it with tears; but the fir tree regarded them not.

Christmas time drew near, and many young trees were cut down, some that were even smaller and younger than the fir tree, who enjoyed neither rest nor peace with longing to leave its forest home. These young trees, which were chosen for their beauty, kept their branches, and were also laid on wagons, and drawn by horses far away out of the forest.

"Where are they going?" asked the fir tree. "They are not taller than I am; indeed, one is not so tall. And why do they keep all their branches? Where are they going?"

"We know, we know," sang the sparrows; "we have looked in at the windows of the houses in the town, and we know what is done with them. Oh! You cannot think what honor and glory they receive. They are dressed up in the most splendid manner. We have seen them standing in the middle of a warm room and adorned with all sorts of beautiful things—honey cakes, gilded apples, playthings, and many hundreds of wax tapers."

"And then," asked the fir tree, trembling in all its branches, "and then what happens?"

"We did not see any more," said the sparrows; "but this was enough for us."

"I wonder whether anything so brilliant will ever happen to me," thought the fir tree. "It would be better even than crossing the sea. I long for it almost with pain. Oh, when will Christmas be here? I am now as tall and well grown as those which were taken away last year. Oh, that I were now laid on the wagon, or standing in the warm room, with all that brightness and splendor around me! Something better and more beautiful is to come after, or the trees would not be so decked out. Yes, what follows will be grander and more splendid. What can it be? I am weary with longing. I scarcely know what it is that I feel."

"Rejoice in our love," said the air and the sunlight. "Enjoy thine own bright life in the fresh air."

But the tree would not rejoice, though it grew taller every day and, winter and summer, its dark green foliage might be seen in the forests, while passersby would say, "What a beautiful tree!"

A short time before Christmas the discontented fir tree was the first to fall. As the axe cut sharply through the stem, and divided the pith, the tree fell with a groan to the earth, conscious of pain and faintness, and forgetting all its dreams of happiness, in sorrow at leaving its home in the forest. It knew that it should never again see its dear old companions, the trees, nor the little bushes and many-colored flowers that had grown by its side, perhaps not even the birds. Nor was the journey at all pleasant.

The tree first recovered itself while being unpacked in the courtyard of a house, with several other trees; and it heard a man say, "We only want one, and this is the prettiest. This is beautiful!"

Then came two servants in grand livery and carried the fir tree into a large and beautiful apartment. Pictures hung on the walls, and near the great stove stood great china vases, with lions on the lids. There were rocking chairs, silken sofas, large tables covered with pictures, books, and playthings that had cost a hundred times a hundred dollars; at least so said the children.

Then the fir tree was placed in a large tub, full of sand; but green baize hung all around it, so that no one could know it was a tub; and it stood on a very handsome carpet. Oh, how the fir tree trembled! What was going to happen to him now? Some young ladies came in, and the servants helped them to adorn the tree.

On one branch they hung little bags cut out of colored paper, and each bag was filled with sweetmeats. From other branches hung gilded apples and walnuts, and all around were hundreds of red, blue, and white tapers, which were fastened upon the branches. Dolls, exactly like real men and women, were placed under the green leaves—and the tree had never seen such things before—and at the top was fastened a glittering star, made of gold tinsel. Oh, it was very beautiful. "This evening," they all exclaimed, "how bright it will be!"

"Oh, that the evening were come," thought the tree, "and the tapers lighted! Then I should know what else is going to happen. Will the trees of the forest come to see me? Will the sparrows peep in at the windows, I wonder, as they fly? Shall I grow faster here, and keep on all these ornaments during summer and winter?" But guessing was of very little use. His back ached with trying; and this pain is as bad for a slender fir tree as headache is for us.

At last the tapers were lighted, and then what a glistening blaze of splendor the tree presented! It trembled so with joy in all its branches, that one of the candles fell among the green leaves and burnt some of them. "Help! help!" exclaimed the young ladies; but there was no danger, for they quickly extinguished the fire.

After this the tree tried not to tremble at all, though the fire frightened him, he was so anxious not to hurt any of the beautiful ornaments, even while their brilliancy dazzled him.

And now the folding doors were thrown open, and a troop of children rushed in as if they intended to upset the tree and were followed more slowly by their elders. For a moment the little ones stood silent with astonishment, and then they shouted for joy till the room rang; and they danced merrily round the tree, while one present after another was taken from it.

"What are they doing? What will happen next?" thought the tree. At last, the candles burned down to the branches, and were put out. Then the children received permission to plunder the tree.

Oh, how they rushed upon it! There was such a riot that the branches cracked, and had it not been fastened with the glistening star to the ceiling, it must have been thrown down.

Then the children danced about with their pretty toys, and no one noticed the tree, except the children's maid, who came and peeped among the branches to see if an apple or a fig had been forgotten.

"A story, a story," cried the children, pulling a little fat man toward the tree.

"Now we shall be in green shade," said the man, as he seated himself under it, "and the tree will have the pleasure of hearing also; but I shall only relate one story. What shall it be? Ivede-Avede, or Humpty-Dumpty, who fell downstairs, but soon got up again, and at last married a princess?"

"Ivede-Avede," cried some. "Humpty-Dumpty," cried others; and there was a famous uproar. But the fir tree remained quite still, and thought to himself, "Shall I have anything to do with all this? Ought I to make a noise too?" but he had already amused them as much as they wished.

Then the old man told them the story of Humpty-Dumpty—how he fell downstairs and was raised up again and married a princess. And the children clapped their hands and cried "Tell another, tell another," for they wanted to hear the story of Ivede-Avede; but this time they had only Humpty-Dumpty. After this the fir tree became quite silent and thoughtful. Never had the birds in the forest told such tales as Humpty-Dumpty who fell downstairs, and yet married a princess.

"Ah, yes! So it happens in the world," thought the fir tree. He believed it all, because it was related by such a pleasant man.

"Ah, well!" he thought, "who knows? Perhaps I may fall down too and marry a princess;" and he looked forward joyfully to the next evening, expecting to be again decked out with lights and playthings, gold and fruit. "Tomorrow I will not tremble," thought he; "I will enjoy all my splendor, and I shall hear the story of Humpty-Dumpty again, and perhaps Ivede-Avede." And the tree remained quiet and thoughtful all night.

In the morning the servants and the housemaid came in. "Now," thought the fir tree, "all my splendor is going to begin again." But they dragged him out of the room and upstairs to the garret and threw him on the floor, in a dark corner where no daylight shone, and there they left him. "What does this mean?" thought the tree. "What am I to do here? I can hear nothing in a place like this;" and he leaned against the wall and thought and thought.

And he had time enough to think, for days and nights passed, and no one came near him; and when at last somebody did come, it was only to push away some large boxes in a corner. So the tree was completely hidden from sight as if it had never existed.

"It is winter now," thought the tree; "the ground is hard and covered with snow, so that people cannot plant me. I shall be sheltered here, I dare say, until spring comes. How thoughtful and kind everybody is to me! Still, I wish this place were not so dark and so dreadfully lonely, with not even a little hare to look at. How pleasant it was out in the forest while the snow lay on the ground, when the hare would run by, yes, and jump over me too, although I did not like it then. Oh! It is terribly lonely here."

"Squeak, squeak," said a little mouse, creeping cautiously towards the tree; then came another, and they both sniffed at the fir tree, and crept in and out between the branches.

"Oh, it is very cold here," said the little mouse. "If it were not, we would be very comfortable here, wouldn't we, old fir tree?"

"I am not old," said the fir tree. "There are many who are older than I am."

"Where do you come from?" asked the mice, who were full of curiosity; "and what do you know? Have you seen the most beautiful places in the world, and can you tell us all about them? And have you been in the storeroom, where cheeses lie on the shelf and hams hang from the ceiling? One can run about on tallow candles there; one can go in thin and come out fat."

"I know nothing of that," said the fir tree; "but I know the wood where the sun shines and the birds sing." And then the tree told the little mice all about its youth. They had never heard such an account in their lives; and after they had listened to it attentively, they said, "What a number of things you have seen! You must have been very happy."

"Happy!" exclaimed the fir tree; and then, as he reflected on what he had been telling them, he said, "Ah, yes! After all, those were happy days." But when he went on and related all about Christmas Eve, and how he had been dressed up with cakes and lights, the mice said, "How happy you must have been, you old fir tree."

"I am not old at all," replied the tree; "I only came from the forest this winter. I am now checked in my growth."

"What splendid stories you can tell," said the little mice. And the next night four other mice came with them to hear what the tree had to tell. The more he talked, the more he remembered, and then he thought to himself, "Yes, those were happy days; but they may come again. Humpty-Dumpty fell downstairs, and yet he married a princess. Perhaps I may marry a princess too." And the fir tree thought of the pretty little birch tree that grew in the forest; a real princess, a beautiful princess, she was to him.

"Who is Humpty-Dumpty?" asked the little mice. And then the tree related the whole story; he could remember every single word. And the little mice were so delighted with it, that they were ready to jump to the top of the tree. The next night a great many more mice made their appearance, and on Sunday two rats came with them; but they said it was not a pretty story at all, and the little mice were very sorry, for it made them also think less of it.

"Do you know only that one story?" asked the rats.

"Only that one," replied the fir tree. "I heard it on the happiest evening of my life; but I did not know I was so happy at the time."

"We think it is a very miserable story," said the rats. "Don't you know any story about bacon or tallow in the storeroom?"

"No," replied the tree.

"Many thanks to you, then," replied the rats, and they went their ways.

The little mice also kept away after this, and the tree sighed and said, "It was very pleasant when the merry little mice sat around me and listened while I talked. Now that is all past too. However, I shall consider myself happy when someone comes to take me out of this place."

But would this ever happen? Yes, one morning people came to clear up the garret; the boxes were packed away, and the tree was pulled out of the corner and thrown roughly on the floor; then the servants dragged it out upon the staircase where the daylight shone.

"Now life is beginning again," said the tree, rejoicing in the sunshine and fresh air. Then it was carried downstairs and taken into the courtyard so quickly that it forgot to think of itself, and could only look about, there was so much to be seen.

The court was close to a garden, where everything looked blooming. Fresh and fragrant roses hung over the little palings. The linden trees were in blossom; while the swallows flew here and there crying, "Twit, twit, twit, my mate is coming;" but it was not the fir tree they meant.

"Now I shall live," cried the tree joyfully, spreading out its branches; but alas! They were all withered and yellow, and it lay in a corner amongst weeds and nettles. The star of gold paper still stuck in the top of the tree and glittered in the sunshine.

In the same courtyard two of the merry children were playing who had danced round the tree at Christmas time and had been so happy. The youngest saw the gilded star and ran and pulled it off the tree. "Look what is sticking to the ugly old fir tree," said the child, treading on the branches till they crackled under his boots.

And the tree saw all the fresh, bright flowers in the garden, and then looked at itself, and wished it had remained in the dark corner of the garret. It thought of its fresh youth in the forest, of the merry Christmas evening, and of the little mice who had listened to the story of Humpty-Dumpty.

"Past! Past!" said the poor tree. "Oh, had I but enjoyed myself while I could have done so! But now it is too late."

Then a lad came and chopped the tree into small pieces, till a large bundle lay in a heap on the ground. The pieces were placed in the fire, and they blazed up brightly, while the tree sighed so deeply that each sigh was like a little pistol shot. Then the children, who were at play, came and seated themselves in front of the fire and looked at it, and cried, "Pop, pop." But at each "pop," which was a deep sigh, the tree was thinking of a summer day in the forest, or of some winter night there when the stars shone brightly, and of Christmas evening and of Humpty-Dumpty, the only story it had ever heard, or knew how to relate—till at last it was consumed.

The boys still played in the garden, and the youngest wore the golden star on his breast with which the tree had been adorned during the happiest evening of its existence. Now all was past; the tree's life was past, and the story also past! For all stories must come to an end sometime or other.

ABOUT THE AUTHOR

HANS CHRISTIAN ANDERSEN (1805–1875) initially strove to be a theater actor but when his soprano voice started changing in his teens, he was encouraged to be a poet instead. Today, the Danish writer is most well-known for his literary fairy tales—156 published throughout his lifetime.

A Bit of History

"The Fir Tree," revolving around an anxious fir tree who can't appreciate living in the moment, serves as a message about deep pessimism. The tree can never see the good in where it currently is and misses out on its youth and health because of its desire to keep moving ahead to bigger and better things. Expressing gratitude for the people and things around us is the most important gift we can give, so while reading "The Fir Tree" this Christmas, make that appreciation known.

"The Fir Tree" was first published in Andersen's anthology *New Fairy Tales. First Volume. Second Collection* in 1844. It has been adapted into several films and television shows since its creation, including *A Charlie Brown Christmas*.

THE BOY WITH THE BOX
By Mary Griggs van Voorhis

It was an ideal Christmas day. The sun shone brightly but the air was crisp and cold, and snow and ice lay sparkling everywhere. A light wind, the night before, had swept the blue, icebound river clean of scattering snow; and, by two o'clock in the afternoon, the broad bend near Creighton's mill was fairly alive with skaters. The girls in gay caps and scarfs, the boys in sweaters and mackinaws of every conceivable hue, with here and there a plump, matronly figure in a plush coat or a tiny fellow in scarlet, made a picture of life and brilliancy worthy of an artist's finest skill.

Tom Reynolds moved in and out among the happy throng, with swift, easy strokes, his cap on the back of his curly head, and his brown eyes shining with excitement. Now and again, he glanced down with pardonable pride, at the brand new skates that twinkled beneath his feet. "Jolly Ramblers," sure enough "Jolly Ramblers" they were! Ever since Ralph Evans had remarked, with a tantalizing toss of his handsome head, that "no game fellow would try to skate on anything but 'Jolly Ramblers,'" Tom had yearned, with an inexpressible longing, for a pair of these wonderful skates. And now they were his and the ice was fine and the Christmas sun was shining!

Tom was rounding the big bend for the fiftieth time, when he saw, skimming gracefully toward him through the merry crowd, a tall boy in a fur-trimmed coat, his handsome head proudly erect.

"That's Ralph Evans now," said Tom to himself. "Just wait till you see these skates, old boy, and maybe you won't feel so smart!" And with slow, cautious strokes, he made his way through laughing boys and girls to a place just in front of the tall skater, coming toward him down the broad white way. When Ralph was almost upon him, Tom paused and in conspicuous silence, looked down at his shining skates.

"Hullo," said Ralph good naturedly, seizing Tom's arm and swinging around. Then, taking in the situation with a careless glance, he added, "Get a new pair of skates for Christmas?"

"'Jolly Ramblers,'" said Tom impressively, "the best 'Jolly Ramblers' in the market!"

Ralph was a full half head the taller, but, as Tom delivered himself of this speech with his head held high, he felt every inch as tall as the boy before him.

If Ralph was deeply impressed he failed to show it, as he answered carelessly, "Huh, that so? Pretty good little skates they are, the 'Jolly Ramblers!'"

"You said no game fellow would use any other make," said Tom hotly.

"O but that was nearly a year ago," said Ralph. "I got a new pair of skates for Christmas, too," he added, as if it had just occurred to him, "'Club House' skates, something new in the market just this season. Just look at the curve of that skate, will you?" he added, lifting a foot for inspection, "and that clamp that you couldn't shake off if you had to! They're guaranteed for a year, too, and if anything gives out, you get a new pair for nothing. Three and a half, they cost, at Mr. Harrison's hardware store. I gave my 'Jolly Ramblers' to a kid about your size. A mighty good little skate they are!" And, with a long, graceful stroke, Ralph Evans skated away.

And it seemed to Tom Reynolds that all his Christmas joy went skimming away behind him. The sun still shone, the ice still gleamed, the skaters laughed and sang, but Tom moved slowly on, with listless, heavy strokes. The "Jolly Ramblers" still twinkled beneath his feet, but he looked down at them no more. What was the use of "Jolly Ramblers" when Ralph Evans had a pair of "Club House" skates that cost a dollar more, had a graceful curve, and a faultless clamp, and were guaranteed for a year?

It was only four o'clock when Tom slipped his new skates carelessly over his shoulder and started up the bank for home. He was slouching down the main street, head down, hands thrust deep into his pockets, when, on turning a corner, he ran plump into—a full moon! Now I know it is rather unusual for full moons to be walking about the streets by daylight; but that is the only adequate description of the round, freckled face that beamed at Tom from behind a great box, held by two sturdy arms.

"That came pretty near being a collision," said the owner of the full moon, still beaming, as he set down the box and leaned against a building to rest a moment.

"Nobody hurt, I guess," said Tom.

"Been down to the ice?" asked the boy, eagerly. "I could see the skaters from Patton's store. O, I see, you got some new skates for Christmas! Ain't they beauties, now?" And he beamed on the despised "Jolly Ramblers" with his heart in his little blue eyes.

"A pretty good little pair of skates," said Tom, in Ralph's condescending tone.

"Good! Well I should guess yes! And Christmas ice just made o' purpose!" In spite of his ill humor, Tom could not help responding to the warm interest of the shabby boy at his side. He knew him to be Harvey McGinnis, the son of a poor Irish widow, who worked at Patton's department store out of school hours. Looking at the great box with an awakening interest, he remarked, kindly, "What you been doin' with yourself on Christmas day?"

"Want to know, sure enough?" said Harvey, mysteriously, his round face beaming more brightly than ever, "Well, I've been doin' the Santy Claus act down at Patton's store.

"About a week ago," he went on, leaning back easily against the tall building and thrusting his hands down deep into his well worn pockets, "about a week ago, as I was cleaning out the storeroom, I came on three big boxes with broken dolls in 'em. Beauties they were, I kin tell you, the Lady Jane in a blue silk dress, the Lady Clarabel in pink, and the Lady Matilda in shimmerin' white. Nothin' wrong with 'em either only broken rubbers that put their jints out o' whack and set their heads arollin' this way and that. 'They could be fixed in no time, I ses to myself, 'and what a prize they'd be fer the kids to be sure!' For mom and me had racked our brains considerable how we'd scrape together the money for Christmas things for the girls.

"So I went to the boss and I asked him right out what he'd charge me for the three ladies just as they wus, and he ses, 'Jimmie,' he ses (I've told him me name a dozen times, but he allus calls me 'Jimmie'), 'Jimmie,' he ses, 'if you'll come down on Christmas day and help me take down the fixins and fix up the store for regular trade, I'll give you the dolls fer nothin',' he ses.

"So I explained to the kids that Santy'd be late to our house this year (with so many to see after it wouldn't be strange) and went down to the store early this morning and finished me work and fixed up the ladies es good es new. Would you like to be seein' 'em, now?" he added, turning to the great box with a look of pride.

"Sure, I'd like to see 'em," said Tom.

With careful, almost reverent touch, Harvey untied the string and opened the large box, disclosing three smaller boxes, one above the other. Opening the first box, he revealed a really handsome doll in a blue silk dress, with large dark eyes that opened and shut and dark, curling locks of "real hair."

"This is the Lady Jane," he said, smoothing her gay frock with gentle fingers. "We're goin' to give her to Kitty. Kitty's hair is pretty and curly, but she hates it, 'cause it's red; and she thinks black hair is the prettiest kind in the world. Ain't it funny how all of us will be wantin' what we don't have ourselves?"

Tom did not reply to this bit of philosophy; but he laid a repentant hand on the "Jolly Ramblers" as if he knew he had wronged them in his heart. "That's as handsome a doll as ever I saw and no mistake," he said.

Pleased with this praise, Harvey opened the second box and disclosed the Lady Matilda with fair golden curls and a dress of "shimmerin' white." "The Lady Matilda goes to Josephine," said Harvey. "Josephine has black hair, straight as a string, and won't she laugh, though, to see them fetchin' yellow curls?"

"She surely ought to be glad," said Tom.

The Lady Clarabel was another fair-haired lady in a gown of the brightest pink. "This here beauty's for the baby," said Harvey, his eyes glowing. "She don't care if the hair's black or yellow, but won't that stunnin' dress make her eyes pop out?"

"They'll surely believe in Santy when they see those beauties," said Tom.

'That's just what I was sayin' to mom this morning," said Harvey. "Kitty's had some doubts, (she's almost nine), but when she sees those fine ladies she'll be dead sure mom and I didn't buy 'em. If I had a Santy Claus suit, I'd dress up and hand 'em out myself."

Tom's face lighted with a bright idea. "My brother Bob's got a Santa Claus suit that he used in a show last Christmas," he said. "Say, let me dress up and play Santa for you. The girls would never guess who I was!"

"Wouldn't they stare, though!" said Harvey, delightedly. "But do you think you'd want to take time," he asked apologetically, "and you with a new pair of skates and the ice like this?"

"Of course, I want to if you'll let me," said Tom. "I'll skate down the river and meet you anywhere you say."

"Out in our back yard, then, at seven o'clock," said Harvey.

"All right, I'll be there!" and with head up, and skates clinking, Tom hurried away.

It was a flushed, excited boy who burst into the Reynolds' quiet sitting room a few minutes later, with his skates still hanging on his shoulder and his cap in his hand. "Say, mother," he cried, "can I have Bob's Santa Claus suit this evening, please? I'm going to play Santa Claus for Harvey McGinnis!"

"Play Santa Claus for Harvey McGinnis. What do you mean, child?"

"You know Mrs. McGinnis, mother, that poor woman who lives in the little house by the river. Her husband got killed on the railroad last winter, you know. Well, Harvey, her boy, has fixed up some grand-looking dolls for his sisters and he wants me to come out and play Santa tonight," and Tom launched out into a long story about Harvey and his good fortune.

"He must be a splendid boy," said Mrs. Reynolds, heartily, "and I am sure I shall be glad to have you go."

"And another thing, mother," said Tom, hesitating a little, "do you think grandma would care if I spent part of that five dollars she gave me for a pair of skates for Harvey? He hasn't any skates at all, and I know he'd just love to have some!"

"It is generous of you to think of it," said his mother, much pleased, "and you would still have two and a half for that little trip down to grandma's."

"But I'd like to get him some 'Club House' skates," said Tom. "They're a new kind that cost three dollars and a half."

"But I thought you said the 'Jolly Ramblers' were the best skates made?" Mrs. Reynolds looked somewhat hurt as she glanced from Tom to the skates on his shoulder and back to Tom again.

"They are, mother, they're just dandies!" said Tom blushing with shame that he could ever have despised his mother's gift. "But these 'Club House' skates are just the kind for Harvey. You see, Harvey's shoes are old and worn, and these 'Club House' skates have clamps that you can't shake loose if you have to. Then, if anything happens to them before the year's up, you get a new pair free; and Harvey, you know, wouldn't have any money to be fixing skates."

"Well, do as you like," said Mrs. Reynolds, pleased with Tom's eagerness, for such a spell of generosity was something new in her selfish younger son. "But remember, you will have to wait a while for your visit to grandma."

"All right, and thank you, mother," said Tom. "You can buy the skates down at Harrison's and I'm going over and ask Mr. Harrison if he won't open up the store and get a pair for me for a special time like this. I'm most sure he will!" and away he flew.

That evening, at seven, as the moon was rising over the eastern hills, a short, portly Santa Claus stepped out of the dry reeds by the river bank and walked with wonderfully nimble feet, right into the McGinnis' little back yard. As he neared the small back porch, a dark figure rose to greet him, one hand held up in warning, the other holding at arm's length, a bulky grain sack, full to the brim.

"Here's yer pack, Santy," he whispered, gleefully. "They're all waitin' in the front room yonder. I'll slip in the back way, whilst you go round and give a good thump at the front door and mom'll let you in."

Trembling with eagerness, Tom tiptoed round the house, managing to slip an oblong package into the capacious depths of the big sack as he did so. Thump, thump! how his knock reechoed in the frosty air! The door swung wide, and Mrs. McGinnis' gaunt figure stood before him.

"Good evenin', Santy, come right in," she said.

Tom had always thought what a homely woman Harvey's mother was when he happened to meet her at the grocery, with her thin red hair drawn severely back from her gaunt face, and a black shawl over her head. But as he looked up into her big, kind face, so full of Christmas sunshine, he wondered he could ever have thought her anything but lovely. The room was small and bare, but wonderfully gay with pine and bits of red and green crepe paper, saved from the 'fixins' at the store. And on a large bed in the corner sat the three little girls, Kitty with her bright curls bobbing, Josephine with her black braids sticking straight out, and the baby with tiny blue eyes that twinkled and shone like Harvey's.

The fine speech that Tom had been saying over to himself for the past two hours seemed to vanish into thin air before this excited little audience. But in faltering, stammering tones, which everyone was too excited to notice, he managed to say something about "Merry Christmas" and "good children" and then proceeded to open the magic sack. "Miss Kitty McGinnis!" he called, in deep, gruff tones. Kitty took the box he offered with shy embarrassment, slowly drew back the lid and gave a cry of amazement and delight. "A doll, O the loveliest doll that ever was!" she cried. Then turning to her brother, she whispered as softly as excitement would permit, "O Harvey, I'm afeard ye paid too much!"

"Aw, go on!" said Harvey, his face more like a full moon than ever. "Don't ye know that Santy kin do whatever he wants to?"

The other dolls were received with raptures, Josephine stroking the golden curls of the Lady Matilda with wondering fingers, and the baby dancing round and round, waving the pink-robed Lady Clarabel above her head.

"Mr. Harvey McGinnis!" came the gruff tones of Santa Claus; and Harvey smiled over to his mother as he drew out a pair of stout cloth gloves.

"Mrs. McGinnis!" And that good lady smiled back, as she shook out a dainty white apron with a coarse embroidery ruffle.

"I reckon Santy wanted you to wear that of a Sunday afternoon," said Harvey, awkwardly.

"And I'll be proud to do it!" said his mother.

Little sacks of candy were next produced and everyone settled down to enjoy it, thinking that the bottom of the big sack must be reached, when Santa called out in tones that trembled beneath the gruffness, "Another package for Mr. Harvey McGinnis!"

"Fer me—why—what—" said Harvey, taking the heavy oblong bundle; then, as the sparkling "Club House" skates met his view, his face lit up with a glory that Tom never forgot. The glory lasted but a moment, then he turned a troubled face toward the bulky old saint.

"You never ought to a done it," he said. "These must have cost a lot!"

"Aw, go on," was the reply in a distinctly boyish tone, "don't you know that Santy can do whatever he wants to?" and, with a prodigious bow, old Santa was gone.

A few minutes later, a slender boy with a bundle under his arm, was skating swiftly down the shining river in the moonlight. As he rounded the bend, a tall figure in a fur-trimmed coat came skimming slowly toward him, and a voice called out in Ralph Evans' condescending tones, "Well, how are the 'Jolly Ramblers' doing tonight?"

But the answer, this time, was clear and glad and triumphant. "The best in the world," said Tom, "and isn't this the glorious night for skating?"

ABOUT THE AUTHOR

The life of **MARY GRIGGS VAN VOORHIS (1800–1900)** is elusive, as "The Boy with the Box" is the only story credited to her name. She is another forgotten author but unlike Helen G. Ricks, her being forgotten is not because of the deliberate exclusion of her work by the literary canon. Rather, van Voorhis' life was simply not well documented. Interestingly, these Christmas stories by the two women were first released in the same year: 1916.

A Bit of History

"The Boy with the Box" first appeared in the 1916 collection *Christmas Stories and Legends* compiled by Phebe A. Curtiss. Curtiss chose stories that carried important morals as well as the Christmas spirit, which "The Boy with the Box" certainly adheres to. The narrator grows from a selfish child preoccupied with looking richer than those around him to both appreciating his own gifts and giving back to another child in need, resulting in a heartwarming evolution of character.